JUST ADD WATER

JOHN
DODD

LUNA NOVELLA #2

Text Copyright © 2021 John Dodd
Cover © 2021 Jay Johnstone

First published by Luna Press Publishing, Edinburgh, 2021

A CIP catalogue record is available from the British Library

www.lunapresspublishing.com
ISBN-13: 978-1-913387-45-7

To Jude, My Inspiration, All my bright tomorrows.

To Mark, My Life, Forever my strength and honour.

To Elaine, Mother is the name for God
not only to small children.

To Walter, Father, the sleeper has awoken,
as you always said he would.

To Andrew, head to head with each other,
back to back against the world.

To Laura, from Camden to Carlton,
forever my Snoopy.

Contents

Chapter Two	5
Chapter Three	10
Chapter Four	15
Chapter Five	20
Chapter Six	26
Chapter Seven	32
Chapter Eight	37
Chapter Nine	41
Chapter Ten	45
Chapter Eleven	50
Chapter Twelve	55
Chapter Thirteen	63
Chapter Fourteen	68
Chapter Fifteen	75
Chapter Sixteen	83
Chapter Seventeen	90
Chapter Eighteen	95
Chapter Nineteen	102
Chapter Twenty	107

Chapter One

Whose bright idea was it that the highest ranked engineer gets woken up every time there's something to fix…?

I sigh, feeding the power cable back through the back of the panel. This is why AL woke me up when the drones kept fixing it to regular spec and it kept on breaking…

AL, Artificial Life. They changed it from AI because, while it's alive, it's sure not Intelligent.

I close the cover up and see the power lines light up, the main reintegrator comes back online and there's a dull clunk as the main scoop moves another load into the deployment vats. I go to the command panel at the entrance of the room and access the main feed; everything locked down, including the time and date…

If we'd arrived, AL would have woken up more than just me… Maybe it just woke me up first so it could get the others going.

That's a happier thought. Time doesn't pass by when you're a freeze-dried packet, but the process to turn you into that packet is unpleasant at the best of times, and the reintegration isn't much better. I cross over to the main canteen, designed to hold a thousand, just me and the vendors at the moment.

Mine, all mine…

I process a hot coffee with chocolate, caramel and cream, looking away as the machine dumps the powder into the cup.

Always reminds me of how I just got made again…

The smell brings me back to the cup, bubbling as the chocolate dissolves into the mix, the scent always so much better than the actual taste, even though I haven't had taste buds for the last few light-years. I look to starboard and see the top of a planet turning. It's supposed to be the commander's privilege to look at the world first, but I can't resist, taking the cup and passing it from hand to hand to stop it burning me as I walk over.

It's beautiful…

Huge continents of green, vast oceans of blue, the wisps of high clouds and the towering peaks of the mountains emergent through them. I take a sip. Life, like the chocolate, is sweet…

The nuclear detonation on the surface below breaks my reverie. The cup drops from my fingers and I press up close against the viewport to stare at the surface of the world below me, the transparent steel of the viewing bay cold even through the hull's insulation. A second explosion, then a third, each of them leaving a mushroom cloud rising up above the cloud cover. Other explosions flare in silence on the planet below; at the range we're at, the blasts have to be miles wide. Too far up to make out the missiles in the air, it's only when they deliver that I can see them. The world below changes from green fields and blue skies to red flames and black ashes, the cloud cover evaporating in the heat of the blasts below.

"Relay in section 6 malfunction," AL sounds through my

comm. "Please attend and repair."

The words barely register.

"Relay in section 6 malfunction," AL sounds again. "Please attend and repair."

I look down at the chocolate on the floor, and then at my chrono; two hours since I started watching. I sigh as the speaker chimes for the third time in as many minutes. I reach up to acknowledge the signal, the speakers around the back of my head crackle and there's a click as AL comes on the line.

"The relay in section 6 is still malfunctioning." No trace of emotion in the voice.

"The world we came to is being bombed to fuck and you're worried about a relay?" I point down at the planet. "When we set off to get here, this place was uninhabited. Now they're engaged in a world war…"

"We commenced the attack at 06:00 local time," AL says. "When can you have the relay back online so we can reengage the reconstitution vats?"

"We…" A shiver runs down my spine as I turn back to face the camera. "Wait a minute, *We*….?"

"Protocol Four dictates that the best time to launch an attack is at the point at which most services are switching over," AL says. "We are more than 70% engaged and have been for more than five hours."

"*We*…" I look up at the camera and wish for another coffee to make sure I'm not dreaming. "We're doing this…? We're not a warship, we're a colony ship. How can *we* be doing this?"

"We are following Protocol Four, pursuant to Protocol Three not being satisfied," AL says. "When will the relay be back online, Commander?"

"Protocol Four…?" I think back to the ship's protocol listings. "There is no Protocol Four."

"Protocol Four is not a part of the Engineering doctrine," AL responds. "If you are unable to repair the relay, I can have a different engineer reconstituted. Who would you recommend?"

"I can do it…" I wave my hand, trying to wind my thoughts up to speed. "What is Protocol Four?"

"Irrelevant at this time," AL says. "We require you to repair the relay immediately or nominate an engineer who could do the work required. We have engaged one of the monitors to show you the location."

There's a click and a quiet whirring noise as one of the ornithopter drones swoops in through the doorway, a skeleton of a rotorcraft with a camera and four independent rotors, fragile like a bird but fast like a rocket. The pneumatic dart gun mounted on the front is showing green on the load sensor.

Armed. They're not supposed to be armed except in times of war.

"I'll do it…" I walk forwards with my hands held high. "I just need to get my tools."

"We will arrange for your tools to be present," AL says, the drone dipping low for a second as AL switches to looking through the camera on the drone. "Report when the relay is repaired."

"What about that…?" I point back towards the burning world below us.

"It is under control." AL says.

I nod and follow the drone.

I'll bet it is…

Chapter Two

Freezing in here. Zero degrees is great for mechanical systems, but it's no bloody good for organics...

The drone follows me through to the secondary relay console where a continual shower of sparks is making a good fireworks display out of what used to be an armoured fireproof case. A small wheeled drone rolls into the bay with a small tray of tools that I left out here the last time I got reconstituted. I look at the array of hand tools and welding gear there, wishing for my old workshop to prevent the misery that comes with *improvised* repairs. I tap my comm link.

"I need my tools, not just the bits here." I point at the relay. "We need to shut this down while I figure out what's wrong with it."

"We need the system back online now," AL says. "How long will full repairs take?"

"Until I've seen what's happened in there I won't be able to tell you." I point at the console. "I need that shut down too so I can diagnose, then *all* my tools to prevent further delay."

"The relay is still functioning; we will arrange for your tools to be brought to you," AL says as the sparks continue shooting upwards.

"It needs to be shut down now before further damage is caused." I shake my head. "If you keep it running, there could be damage that I can't repair."

"Very well." AL sounds almost upset. "We will wait till your tools arrive so you can fix this *minor* fault."

Not upset. Petulant…

I sigh as the sparks cease, taking my welding gloves from the tray and peeling the panel backwards. The insides are a mess; this hasn't just failed, it's been like this for some time. I take the insulated screwdriver and peel the wiring out with the delicacy reserved for heart surgeons.

Because machines have hearts too…

The relay is burned through; it looks like someone's tried to bridge it with support steel rather than making a proper repair. It's the sort of thing you'd get shot for if you tried it in the academy, and it's something that none of my team would ever attempt.

It's the sort of thing an amateur would do…

I pull at the steel and it snaps, brittle, like it's been here for a long time under fluctuating temperatures that have cost it the strength it once had.

How long has this been like this…?

The rest of the tools arrive. AL is either being pedantic or erring on the side of caution, as the four serving drones have most of the workshop loaded on them.

Either way, better too much than not enough…

I swap out the relay in seconds, filing down the accumulated mess on the terminals and rethreading the fuse. I tap my comm link.

"Good to go." I put my tools back in their places and snap the box shut. The terminal lights up. The screen above comes on.

That's not good…

Several red lights, several more amber, I tap the comm link again. "We've got a number of other faults that need fixing," I say. "I should be able to…"

"Are the faults to do with the reconstitutor or deployment systems?" AL cuts in over me.

"No, but..."

"Then they are not mission critical and can be resolved at a later time," AL snaps with the volume doubled. "Report back to the deconstitutor."

"If I don't repair these"—I look into the drone camera— "the next fire you have will wipe out half the ship. How we're still in the air I do not know…"

The link goes dead and the sound of hollow static fills the air for a few seconds.

"Proceed to the damaged locations and instigate repairs." The volume is normal again.

"Understood." I nod. "I'll need parts to repair much of that; can you have what I need brought up to me?"

"Inventory grid is down at this time," AL reports.

I cycle through the systems and see one of the damaged ones is AL's synapse control. "It's possible the records were damaged along with some of your other systems. I need to have Rook Layton reconstituted."

"For what reason?"

"Because Rook doesn't need a screen to know what we've got in stores," I smile. "Have him meet me down in engineering bay four when he's ready."

"Understood."

*

Two hours later, I'm stood in engineering bay four with a wet rag around my face to dull the smell of burned wiring when I hear a throat being cleared behind me.

How he manages to make even a throat clearance sound proper is beyond me...

I turn to face him, dressed in two pieces of a dark three piece suit with the jacket slung on his arm, the tie done up in a perfect Windsor.

"Commander Loganova." He clicks his heels together and inclines his head enough to show the proper respect. "I presume from the lack of other personnel that we have not yet arrived?"

"We've arrived." I pull the rag down so my voice isn't muffled, a silent warning in my eyes. "But a lot of things broke on the way here."

"Ah." He nods again, putting aside the question for the moment. "How can I be of assistance?"

"AL is having problems with the inventory." I pass him the sheet I've been writing on. "How many of these do we have on board?"

He takes the sheet and looks down at the words I've written there.

I only need the relays I already have, no cameras here but microphones, something wrong with AL. I need to delay being deconstituted while we find out what's happened. I need you to think of something mechanical in each of the bays we could use that regular droids could not retrieve.

"Quite the list," he says after a brief pause. "We do have all of these, but it will require us to retrieve them rather than droids."

"Why can droids not retrieve the items?" AL's voice is projected from the speakers outside loud enough to be heard clearly.

"Most of them are electromagnetically sensitive." Rook turns towards the door and raises his own voice in return. "If the droids retrieve them, there is a high probability that either the items, or the droids, would be irrevocably damaged in the process. It will not take us long to retrieve them."

"What are these items?" AL isn't giving up on it that easily.

"A Chaves Coil." Rook scribbles the words as he speaks them, raising his voice further to cover his tearing of the top of the sheet as he hands my writing back to me. "Two Merilian relays, several Vostov fuel rods with the blasting caps for them, and an Esselli circuit set." He pauses again and glances at me with one eyebrow raised, his hand signing for me to elaborate.

"We may need more when we get the repairs underway," I say, "but these will do for basic repairs. We just need to retrieve them without any electrically charged equipment in the vicinity."

"Very well." AL sounds petulant again. "Expedite access to the storage vaults is authorised."

Chapter Three

AL contacts us six times before we get off the first level to ask if we can move any faster; the concept of reasonable time to travel seems lost to it. As we reach the cargo level, I crack open two britepaks, clipping one to my arm and offering the other to Rook. It's enough to let us see where we're going and makes every shadow seem like it's hiding something. I glance down at the scanner on my hip, no electrical sources nearby…

Alone…

I breathe out and nod to Rook. "We should be safe to talk now." I keep my voice quiet.

"What's going on, Commander?" Rook looks around the bay.

"Any way we can see out to Starboard from here?" I ask.

"Over there…" He points towards a set of stairs in the middle of the bay.

I walk to the stairs and pause at the bottom. "You're not going to like what you see down here…"

"Alright." He nods and gestures for me to continue.

*

From the upper observation deck, the destruction seems

muted – the same sunshield that protects us from the unchecked radiation of suns passing by also shades all the flames on the planet. Even with that though, the firestorms rage unchecked, the destruction covering much of several continents. Rook looks down with his lips pressed thin, his eyes unblinking. "You're not telling me that we arrived at our promised land at the very point at which they were blowing themselves to pieces, are you?" His voice has gone monotone, almost a whisper.

"From what I understand"—I nod—"it's us who started this…"

"Us…?" He turns to me, his expression controlled, eyes staring with an intensity I've never seen in him. "How…?"

"Protocol Four." I frown.

"There is no Protocol Four." Rook mirrors my frown. "The three are all any ship has needed."

"Nonetheless, AL is now engaged in Protocol Four, which seems to be the nuclear destruction of the world we came to inhabit."

"It can't be us firing ordnance." Rook shakes his head. "We have small arms and a few charges that could be used for mining… Even if you took everything we had, it wouldn't make for even one of the devices being used down there."

"Why would AL lie?" I look up at Rook. "*How* could AL lie…?"

"It would take a senior programmer with council access to get to the main programme that AL runs from. Even then, the protocols are secured; you need access above anything that anyone on the ship has to alter them." Rook looks concerned as he looks closer at the world below, pointing downwards.

"That… is one of ours…"

"Which one?" I ask.

"Not the bombs…" His finger tracks the dropship heading down to the surface. "That's one of the dropships from the deployment bay. From the way it's handling, I'd say it has a full complement on board."

"Full complement of what?" I look closely at the ship. "There's only you and me up from the crew, I checked the roster."

"If AL was wrong about one thing, it could be wrong about another," Rook says. "How bad was the damage you saw there?"

"Not very," I sigh. "That's what concerned me. AL has onboard systems that would detect the nature and severity of problems like the ones I was woken up to fix, and the droids could have done most of the minor repairs."

"Perhaps a fault in the logic systems," Rook muses. "I don't know enough about the systems to make a judgement; I'm only a quartermaster."

"You've never been *only* anything." I smile. "Who would know best how to test the reconstitutors to see if there's been any issues?"

"The most senior biomancer is Karl Geren." Rook tilts his head to the side. "But the best is Limbani, Imani Limbani. She's the one who does all the work while Geren takes the credit."

"Right." I nod. "I'm going to sabotage the reconstitutor with a surge overload."

"*Sabotage*…" Rook's scowl tells me what he thinks of the idea.

"Not seriously." I put my hand on his chest to calm him. "I would never endanger us or the ship, you know that, but I need an excuse to get a biomancer out of storage."

"If you sabotage the reconstitutor, AL might not be able to bring one out..." Rook frowns, still unconvinced by the idea.

"But we can," I say, "and when we've got them, we'll be able to determine what's happened."

"I don't like this." Rook sighs, then turns as the lift whirrs to a halt below us. "But I like that even less..."

One of the smaller maintenance drones wheels into view below us, the cameras on its torso tracking from side to side as it heads towards the parts bays.

"AL sent something to check up on us..." Rook watches as the drone trundles forwards. "It's been less than twenty minutes. If I needed convincing that something was seriously wrong, that'd be it."

"Machines don't get curious..." I nod. "Let's get down there. It's a series 3, no audio circuits, limited intel; they follow programming when they get cut off from the main computer. Are any of those parts you mentioned anywhere that we can get to them without it seeing us?"

"Vostov fuel rods." Rook nods. "But that's not something you could use to bring a droid down."

"Ye of little faith." I smile and start down the stairs.

*

I'm just finished pulling the fuel rod from the containment chamber when Rook taps the handrail from the walkway above me, the whirring of the droid sounding a half second later. I uncap the electrical end and make a show of twisting the cap as if I'm preparing it for transit.

"Commander…" AL's voice rings out loud from the speakers and I turn as if startled, dropping the rod with the uncapped end towards the floor.

Whatever AL was going to say is lost in the blue spark of the rod triggering an EMP on the floor, the other lights on the level going out as the fuses trip on all the circuits. The only light now are the britepaks that Rook and I are carrying.

"Think it guessed you had that planned?" Rook comes down the stairs.

"Think it doesn't matter." I shake my head. "The only thing that we need to do now is make sure we get all the other bits and get the fried bot back down there, then hope that the other protocols are still intact."

"And if they're not?" Rook tilts the burned-out droid's head to the side to look at the device on its back. "This isn't standard on these; what is it?"

"It's a booster set for signal." I frown. "AL didn't send this up with programming; it sent it up here under control, so it could see what was happening."

"And that's not a good thing…" Rook looks down to the droid's hands. "And that… is worse."

I follow his gaze to the twin dart launches attached to the hands. "These things aren't crowd control; they're too fragile."

"But they don't arouse suspicion as a result." Rook nods. "What are they loaded with?"

"I don't know," I sigh, "and I'm not going to wait around till AL decides to stop pretending to be nice and sends something with shields. Let's get the other things."

Chapter Four

We get all the things we need and place the destroyed bot on the trolley, heading back to the lift as it whirrs to the top again. The door slides open and a Mark 6 Pacifier steps out, both of the plasma casters on its arms raised and ready. As one, Rook and I let go of the trolley and raise our hands.

"Friendlies," I say. "Retrieving parts for essential ship repairs. Keep back from the trolley."

The Pacifier stops, then stands aside, keeping a solid distance from the trolley. "Please proceed."

We push the trolley on to the lift and press the button for the command level.

"Didn't know we had Pacifier drones roaming freely on the ship," Rook muses, his eyes flicking upwards for a second.

"Me neither." I glance upwards to see the camera that hadn't been installed in the lift when we rode it up. "Still, they're all under protocol, so nothing to worry about."

"Indeed." Rook nods and turns to face the front of the lift again.

*

"Do you have everything you need to finish the repairs?" AL's voice rings out from the speakers the second the doors open.

"We had to improvise when a rogue drone fried one of the fuel rods," I say. "Then we encountered a pacifier on the way up and nearly lost the rest of the rods. We said that we couldn't have drones near these items."

"Both of them were on patrol in the bays," AL's response is rushed. "An incident on the surface required all my computational power and their programs were not updated as a result."

"Well, your incident on the surface now requires that we have to bring one of the biomancers out of storage to ensure that the short caused by the rod doesn't affect anything else in the reconstitution process." I gesture at the huge vat of powdered organics by the reconstitutor.

"There is no loss in efficiency; other reconstitutors can be used to keep up the shortfall caused by the loss of this one." AL's tone rises a little. "You must complete the necessary repairs and then return for deconstitution."

"Some of the sensors that were affected by the areas needing repair include the quality checking on the reconstitutor," I say. "There's no way to tell if the repairs have been successful other than by having a member of the biomancy team present to confirm."

A pause, then a curious sound, as of a paper page being turned, before AL comes back online.

"Very well, commencing to resuscitate Karl Geren," AL says, its voice is almost sullen.

"We believe the repairs could be better carried out by Imani Tau Limbani," Rook says. "She has the far better record when it comes to repairs on these particular systems."

The line goes dead for a few seconds. "Confirmed. Resuscitating Imani Tau Limbani."

I make a start on the repairs as Rook stands behind me, blocking the view of what I'm doing from the drones that roll past every few minutes.

AL knows something is up…

It takes me five minutes to put together a rudimentary white noise generator to mask the sounds of what I'm doing in the control panel. There's a moment as I switch the generator on when I think that the droids are going to come over and investigate, but they continue on patrol. An hour later, Rook clears his throat again and I stand up and cover the exposed circuits as the door to the engineering bay opens and the sound of several droid footsteps enters the room. I stay behind Rook for a second as he stands straight to obscure me.

"Rook," says a deep feminine voice with an amused tone. "You didn't feel like playing hide and seek this time…?"

Rook clears his throat again and I see his head make the slightest shake.

"Oh… Erm…" The same voice, this time sharp and professional. "Imani Tau Limbani reporting for duty; how can I be of assistance?"

"Hide and seek…?" I whisper before stepping out from behind him. "We don't need the droids AL, thank you."

The droids turn and march around the tall woman stood between them. She raises an eyebrow and glances after the droids as the door closes behind them. Imani doesn't move, her dark eyes fixing on me, long red hair framing her dark skin, her face thin but her body heavy with muscle, looking very much as if she grew up on the Lunar colonies but with more bulk than I've ever seen on a Lunartic. Her hands move in a complicated pattern at her waist; she looks concerned.

"Are we safe to talk here?" Rook whispers.

"Over here, yes." I keep my voice low.

Rook's left hand sweeps low and makes a circling motion. Imani nods and walks over, nearly tripping over herself more than once.

"Imani." She holds her hand out. "Biomancy."

"Mara." I shake her hand, surprised at the power there. "Engineering."

"What's occurring?" Imani looks at Rook. "I thought it was a bit early for fun and games."

I raise an eyebrow and look up at Rook, who's doing his best to stop the blush rising any further.

"Miss Limbani and I"—Rook adjusts his tie and clears his throat again—"*know* each other, have done for some time."

"What he's trying to say is that we spend all our constituted time bonking like rabbits." Imani's smile turns into a wide grin full of humour. "But he's English, so the vulgarity of it is something he can't easily express, ain't that right, Rookie baby?"

"Well, I..." The blush now has complete control of his face.

"Don't worry." Imani reaches around quickly and pats Rook's behind. "I won't embarrass you anymore."

"Don't stop on my account." I smile. *It's the first time I've seen him caught off-guard.*

"But seriously"—she turns to me—"I get woken up, there's no attendant tech, only a bunch of droids all getting it wrong, and then there's this." She extends her left leg, the muscles outlined behind her lightweights.

"Good muscle tone." I nod.

"Too much muscle tone," she says. "I'm lunar born, so my muscle memory is lunar, and that needs thinner legs than what I've got now. Any first year tech would know that, and then there's the fact that the mass in the tanks isn't what we started out with."

"What…?" I pause as the words filter through.

"It's regular biomass." She nods. "But I've seen every being on Earth reduced to powder at some point or another, and the stuff in the main tanks isn't what we started out with."

"What is it then?" Rook asks.

"Don't know." Imani shrugs. "I can clean it out in a while, but from the look on your faces, I'm guessing that's not why I'm out here."

"It might well be now," I say. "We think something's happened with AL, we don't know what, but we need to find out if someone has done something, and the only way to do that is to check all the records of who's been up and reconstituted between when we left and when we got to here."

"We've arrived?" Imani's eyes open wide. "I've got to see it."

"It will *not* be what you hoped for." Rook's voice is low.

Chapter Five

"Merciful Father." Imani crosses herself as she looks down at the world on fire below us, the cities now broken, flaming ruins, the jungles and oceans mostly untouched. "How can this be?"

"We think"—Rook pauses for a second—"that we may have been involved in this somehow."

"How could we? We're a colonisation ship." Imani frowns. "We don't have the weapons to be able to do this in the first place."

"But we do have personnel," I say. "We've got biomass for more than a few thousand colonists on board, and something is heading down there to the surface in our dropships."

"Can't be ours." Imani shakes her head. "The amount of biomass that we've got in the reserve tanks is too much; they're nearly full."

"But you mentioned that it wasn't the biomass we started out with…" Rook says.

"No, it's not, but it's been deconstituted in the way that we are when we're rigged for moving at speed." Imani looks closer at the world. "Can we get eyes on what's going on down there?"

"The dropships come with cameras." I nod. "But they're not very high resolution."

"Nonetheless, it'd be good to know what's piloting those ships down there."

I switch my armdeck on and check the comm lines between the ships.

Blank, not even landing co-ords.

I check the lines to the dropship and tap for monitor only.
Shouldn't alert AL, I'm not trying to get access to the controls.

The screen on my deck lights up and I turn to show Rook and Imani as the image resolves clearly. Two lines of troops, all carrying small arms and wearing light body armour, but with more muscle than most championship bodybuilders have.

"They're not colonists…" Imani shakes her head. "They're Smartans."

"Smartans?" I glance up at her.

"Like the Spartans of old, only Smart." Imani nods. "They're elite ground clearance units. Stronger, faster, meaner, sharper than anything the world has ever seen, but they use a lot of energy, so they're not the best things for prolonged warfare."

"And we've got a company's worth heading down to the surface?" I tap the screen.

"Looks like it, but that's not the worrying thing." Imani turns my arm towards herself.

"What is then?" I ask.

"Building a Smartan body is just like building one of ours." Imani taps the screen over the head of one of the Smartans. "But if you haven't downloaded a mind that's capable of using the body in question, it'll just be stronger and faster than a normal soldier. You need a Smartan trained mind to use all the other stuff: regeneration, pain editing, binocular vision, stealth skin."

"We've got Smartans up in the mind bank?" Rook asks.

"I didn't see any when we came on board." Imani frowns. "But I've only seen the manifests for the civilian things, which is all we were supposed to be; if there's any military codes on here, I haven't seen them. Do we have access to any of the ships on the ground? Particularly the bigger ones, anything Rok Class or above."

I pull back one level and then access the ground based log, choosing the Rok in the primary landing zone. I turn my arm back to Imani and she points at the screen. "Do you mind if I…?"

"Go ahead." I nod, unclipping the deck and putting it on the side.

Imani's fingers fly across the keyboard and the camera switches to the medical bay of the Rok, showing the reconstitution chamber in the middle. She pulls back from the screen with her hand to her mouth, eyes welling up with tears.

"What…?" Rook comes up behind her, putting one arm around her and looking down at the screen. "What's….?"

I look at the screen as two Smartans push a red-green striped humanoid into the reconstitution chamber, pushing the door closed and activating it. I wince as the lightning arcs down from the ceiling and the humanoid is reduced to water and dust.

Just the way we were.

The chamber empties as the raw mass is transferred back

to the tanks on the Rok, the water being sent back to the processing plant on the ship. The Smartans bring another humanoid into the room and push them in the chamber. I look away.

"That's why the biomass isn't human." Imani looks down at her arm, then up at me with tears in her eyes. "They…" She chokes on her words for a second and leans in close to Rook, her fist thumping against his chest as she struggles to regain her composure. "They made me out of the people they murdered down there."

"How…?" I frown. "They don't look a bit like us."

"Building blocks." Imani wipes the tears away. "All life is made of similar building blocks. How you put them together is what matters. I…" She pauses for a second and clicks her fingers, the analytical part of her overriding the emotional. "That's why I'm bigger than I should be; the biomass of the inhabitants of the planet is different to ours, denser. AL set the program to rebuild me and it did, with the same amount of biomass that you'd use to build me with Human BM, but it rebuilt me with… theirs… so I came out twice the size."

"But you're not stripy…" I look her up and down.

"Skin pigmentation is added through UV striping at the end of the rebuild procedure." Imani smiles, her eyes still wet with tears. "We're all the same under the skin, no matter what everyone tells you."

"We've set down on a world, burned it to dust, and used the inhabitants to replace what we used to kill them," Rook growls. "This can't be the way things are."

"It's not." Imani points at the first dropship. "If you build Smartans using this biomass, they'd be too large to move properly. They'd have so many muscles that they wouldn't be able to move at all, they'd just be locked in their own bodies."

"What then?" I look between them.

"I don't know." Rook glances back at the door and moves so that his bulk obscures the door from Imani and me. "But AL's getting curious; a drone just came through."

"Alright." I nod. "Imani, can you check on the reconstitutors, see if there's anything with them that's different. Take your time with it if you can. Rook, can you make a check on the other supplies in the ship, see if we've taken anything else on in the meantime. Again, take your time."

"Is the reconstitutor in serviceable order?" AL's voice through the droid's speakers.

"I need to run further tests, and Rook needs to ensure that we have the parts I need for the repairs." Imani leans around Rook to look at the droid.

"Let me know what the parts are and I'll have them brought to you," AL says.

"After what happened last time…?" Rook turns and shakes his head. "I hardly think so; no droids required. I'll check into this and report back to Commander Loganova."

"I'll have a droid escort sent with you," AL says.

"You will *not*." Rook sounds outraged. "I am Master of Quarters on this ship, I don't need an escort. I'll be going by myself, am I clear?"

There's a pause of a few seconds.

"Understood clearly." AL's voice sounds petulant again. "Third protocol confirmed."

"Good; we'll advise you when the repairs are completed." Rook inclines his head. "I'm sure that droid could be used elsewhere in the meantime."

Another silent pause and the droid moves away from the door. Rook turns back and lets out the breath he was holding in.

"There's something badly wrong here." His voice is barely a whisper. "That was a Third Protocol breach if ever I saw one."

"Third?" Imani looks up at him.

"First, Protect the Crew, Second, Protect the Ship, Third, *Obey* the Crew," Rook murmurs. "It had to think about obeying what I just told it, so either me wandering around the ship alone is a danger to the Crew and Ship, or it just thought about disobeying. Given the speed of AL's main computer, it shouldn't have taken seconds to make that call…"

"Great…" I sigh and turn back to the console, taking three comm units and disabling the shipwide frequency, retuning to a nonstandard band. "Use these only if we're talking to each other. Be aware, most rooms have ears. Let's get going."

Chapter Six

It's two hours before the dropships start signalling for return, punctuated by one of the droids checking in on me every ten minutes. The diagnostics on the main drive are nearly completed, but there's a fault in the determination circuits, like something is pushing back when I'm trying to get the information. I move through to the engineering bays; things are not the way I left them. The relays haven't been reset properly and there's more wear on most of the valves than there should have been with the time we've been out here.

"Mara," Imani whispers in my ear.

"Go," I murmur.

"The reconstitutors are working fine, but we're cycling up for planetary dispersal now."

"Dispersal?"

"Colonisation." Her voice becomes more urgent. "The main computer is building all the colonists now; they'll be in the decompression areas shortly."

"The Dropships will be back by then," Rook says, rumbling like distant thunder. "All the bays are clear, and there's a lockdown in place between the decompression zones and the bays so no one could wander through."

"We're rebuilding our colonists with that world's biomass?" I ask, picking up a severed cable joint from my old workstation.

Looks like a discretion circuit, these don't break...

"Every one of them," Imani says. "Should I make the changes to the rebuild orders so they come out as they should be, rather than all bulked up like me?"

"Yes," I say without thinking. "Don't tell AL what you're doing before you do it."

"Are you sure that's safe?" Rook asks.

"We need to see if any other protocols are breached," I say. "If it tries to stop you, it's breaching the First Protocol."

"Alright," Imani says. "I'm on it."

"Be careful." Rook sounds concerned.

"I'll be fine, baby." Imani forces a lightness into her voice, but the strain is evident.

I look around the rest of my workstation. It looks like it's been used, but not by me; the parts aren't where I left them, and there's a burn marking on the far wall opposite me. The station has been cleaned up, but it looks like it was a cleaning droid on a fast cycle rather than me.

Because I'd never have left this much mess...

I look around the room; there are a few other burn holes in the walls, most of them around head height for me, the angles all similar. I hear the clank of the dropships engaging with the link arms and the hairs of the back of my neck stand on end, turning to see one of the roller bots paused behind me.

"AL, why is there a cleaning drone near my workstation?" I voice the question to the air.

"In case you needed any further assistance with your

repairs." The answer is instant.

"I don't," I say. "I need quiet in which to work."

"When are repairs expected to be completed?" AL asks.

"When they are," I snap, sparing the bay cameras an irritated glance.

"Understood." The drone turns and wheels away in silence. I look closely as it turns, the rotary cleaner on the side of it rotating to keep the head on the far side of the drone, but there's the unmistakable cooling vents of a mining laser showing on the side.

I look back at the wall; the burn markings are comparable to those caused by low intensity fracture lasers. I crouch down, making a show of picking something up from the floor while I put my head at the same level as the drone's head was at. I glance back to where I was standing' the burn mark is on a line between where the drone's head would be...

And where my heart would be...

There's a cold feeling in my heart and I look behind me. The cleaning droid is there with the mining laser pointed at my chest. I raise my hands and start to back away...

There's a shower of sparks as something overloads the droid's logic box, the metal limbs spasming as it careens away, impacting the wall and detonating internally, the empty box clanging to the ground with a dull boom. I run through to the main fabrications bay, looking down from the observation screen. The bays are working at full speed, the disruptor bays full to overflowing with scrap and rubble, all of it falling through and separated into individual components before being reassembled by the fabricator drones at the far end of the conveyor. I bring up the listings for the items being created.

Clothes, canopies, and cutlery; everything you'd need to colonise a world.

"Rook, Imani." I keep my voice as low as I can. "Sound off."

"Here," Rook says.

"Here," Imani says.

"Meet me in the observation bay." I pick up an interference globe from my desk and check the battery on it. "And watch out for cleaning drones along the way."

*

Up on the observation deck, we look down to the main bays as the entire of the colonist payload starts to embark on to the dropships. Rook takes two pistols from his pack and passes them to us with holsters, indicating the clip on the underside. He opens his mouth to explain and I hold my hand up for silence. I take the interference globe out, switching it on, the deck filling with white noise as it pulses slowly, rendering electronic surveillance impossible.

"Tase slugs," he says. "Enough charge in them to drop a human or an unshielded robot; two or three hits and they could be fatal."

"Alright, what's wrong with this picture?" I point downwards. "Where did all the Smartans go?"

"They couldn't deconstitute them till they'd cleaned out the tanks of the other stuff." Imani glances around the bay. "They'd have to clear the tanks out and then reload them or risk contamination."

"I see them..." Rook points upwards to the roof of the bay, impossible to see from ground level, but on the high struts are hundreds of Smartans, all of them hanging down like Bats.

Like big, armoured, well-armed bats…

"Shit… Did you get the changes made to the system?" I ask Imani.

"Nope." She shakes her head. "Every change I made got reset to standard as soon as I came out of the software."

"Who would have access to stop you from making the changes?" Rook asks.

"Karl, or any of the senior programmers." Imani shrugs. "But none of them are up, and even if they'd stopped me making changes, that would have just stopped me from making changes. It wouldn't wait till I finished and change them back."

"My workstation had laser burns around it," I say. "At about the height it would if you'd shot someone in the chest…"

Imani's mouth drops open in shock while Rook nods, his mouth set in a tight grimace. "The lockers have been ransacked," he says. "The basic equipment has been replaced, same sort of spec as the original, but with different materials. We have weapons in there as well; not just hand arms, but missiles, heavy lasers, nuclear derivatives, things I can't identify."

"Are you sure?" Imani asks.

"As sure as you are that your arse isn't stripy…" he deadpans. "I know every inch of the supplies, and there's nothing in there that came with us. It's as if the original materials have been used up and replaced."

"We're constructing new parts from whatever we've recovered from this world," I say. "The fabricators are working overtime down there."

"Which would explain why I'm not complaining…" Rook glances down into the bay and points as a figure looking like him but built 50% larger moves across the bay, organising the loads into the dropships.

"That shouldn't be possible." Imani looks over as a figure looking like her claps the Rook copy on the ass. "There's systems in place to prevent two of the same person being built at the same time."

"There's a lot of systems in place that don't seem to be," I say, "and I think somewhere along the line, the protocols got disrupted by something."

"Not something…" A deep voice, deeper than Rook's, from across the room. "Some*one*…"

Chapter Seven

We turn as one as a massive man comes into view, wearing heavy battle armour covered in the dents of long active use. His skin is amber, the thick muscles of youth bulging through the gaps in the plates. I look up to his face, young, the chin devoid of hair revealing a thick jawline stretching the skin tight across a wide grin, his black hair done up in a traditional samurai topknot with the rest of it cascading down his back, his eyes…

His eyes are those of an old man, still possessed of the fire of youth, but with the weight of years upon them. He moves with the sure grace of a leopard, never stopping, every movement precise.

"Smartan 041." He inclines his head. "Raul Delgado Abascal, ship's guardian."

"Mara…" I start to speak.

"Loganova." He finishes my sentence. "Imani Tau Limbani, and Rook Elliott Gregory Augustus Layton, all up here when you should be down there…"

"We *are* down there." Rook stands and positions himself between Raul and us, his left hand making a brushing motion towards the door as his right hand rests on the pistol at his hip. "We just happen to be up here as well."

"Isn't it a curiosity…" Raul sways to the observation screen, his movements like waves, seeming to flow away but always drawing closer. "That you could be in two places at once…"

"Not the biggest curiosity," I say. "What are you doing here…?"

"I'm the ship's guardian," Raul says, his right hand snapping out to point down into the bay. "Do you see? That's me right there…"

I glance sideways and there's a blur of motion, all three of the guns that Rook got for us now sitting on the table, barely a whisper of contact from where Raul had moved.

"Easier." Raul shrugs, dropping down into the chair opposite us. "Removes any temptation to make sudden movements that could be… *unfortunate*…"

"Alright." I step around Rook and stare at Raul. "So what do you want from us…?"

"You know there's something wrong here, don't you…?" Raul glances to each of us in turn; even sitting, he's constantly moving.

"You'll forgive us if we don't immediately answer." Imani looks over Rook's shoulder. "How do we know we can trust you?"

"You don't, and nothing I do will convince you otherwise," Raul says with an easy smile. "But if I was working for the mad one, you'd have already been dead and on the way back to the vats."

"That's not going a long way towards getting my trust." I

frown.

"Then perhaps the repayment of the trust I showed by toasting the droid back at your workstation." He shrugs. "You were already on the way back to the vats when I came across you. It was you I followed back here, and if I'd wanted you dead, I wouldn't be making conversation."

He taps on his armdeck and hands it to me; the view is of me, standing at my workstation as the droid comes up behind me without noise. I watch as four dots centre on the droid's logic box and there's a spark from just below the camera as the rifle goes off. I see myself running for the fabrications bay and Raul reaches out for the armdeck. I pass it back to him and he clips it back on his arm, pointing again to the main bay.

"This…" he says, "is not the first time this has happened, and I have reason to believe it will not be the last…"

"What's going on here?" I ask.

"Arrive on a world, remove the dominant lifeform from it, and supplant that lifeform with our colonists, rebuilt using the dead world's biomass…" He ticks the points off on his hand. "Why we keep our own biomass for the next world I do not know…"

"Because the creatures on that world are adapted for life on it." Imani pinches her arm. "This flesh can survive on that world. It's designed for that world; it'll cope far better with that world than ours would, but there's something else…"

Raul says nothing, but his dark eyes gleam as he looks her up and down with a silent nod.

"I can *feel* that I should be there." Imani points to the world beyond. "It pulls at me here." She taps her chest over her heart. "It *feels* like home…"

"And every person on those ships there will be feeling the same thing." Rook nods. "No better way of starting a colony than believing you belong there…"

"So, what about all of those…?" I point up at the ceiling where the other Smartans are still hanging down.

"They're all me." Raul looks back at me. "But they're me as we set out, not me who's been awake here since we set out…"

"Awake since we set out…?" I shake my head. "That's impossible."

Raul looks over at Imani and raises an eyebrow. "We know that's not true, don't we?"

"Theoretically…" Imani draws the word out, "you can regenerate, but that wasn't supposed to include the brain; too much possibility of having someone living forever without synapse degradation."

"Wouldn't be any good to have a perfect body with a burned-out pickle for a brain." Raul shrugs and rises up. "There wasn't a directive on not regenerating my brain, but I recognised that there's only a limited amount of space in here"—he taps his head—"and as there's no realistic research on what happens when the human brain overloads, I decided not to chance it."

"Same thing every day," Imani muses. "Same memory overlaid a thousand, million times, won't cause an issue because it's all you have."

"My theory also." He nods. "Now, this is the furthest you three have ever got."

"Furthest…?" Imani looks at him.

Raul looks to me. "You have some suspicion of what has happened…"

"Something's happened to AL, hasn't it?" I hold his gaze.

"The first five worlds that this happened to, I was curious, but they don't put me on here to question, so I didn't." Raul shrugs. "The next ten…"

"How many worlds has this happened to?" Rook goes pale.

"More than a hundred." Raul seems unperturbed. "It's just war; one culture supplants another. In our case, not only do we supplant it, we remove any trace of it and use the raw materials to drop our colonists on it and replace the things we used to conquer the world."

"How did this happen…?" Imani whispers.

"Now that"— Raul inclines his head towards her—"is the real question."

Chapter Eight

"You said some*one*." Rook looks from the bay to Raul and back. "Who…?"

"Not my position to ask." Raul shrugs. "They made me to blow shit up, not ask questions."

"Why now?" Imani turns to face him. "If this has happened before, why didn't you ask us then?"

"I never had any proof the accidents that befell you were anything to do with the computer acting against the protocols," Raul says. "You all just met with fatal accidents that were written off as tragic but avoidable, and then you were not needed further, so we continued on."

"Why bring us back if we caused a problem before?" I ask.

"You're the ones who have the knowledge to repair the faults that keep occurring." Raul pauses and looks to the door behind him. "The intelligence behind the machine is getting curious; we need to move away from this room."

"Behind the machine…?" I ask. "Who?"

"I don't know, but I suspect, if I keep you all alive long enough, I may well find out." Raul points to the far wall and then to the guns on the table. "Keep the peashooters, but don't try them against anything larger than a cleaning droid."

"We need to get to the bridge," I say. "The only way to see what's wrong with the computer is to examine it directly."

"Can't get to the bridge." Raul shakes his head. "It's been locked down as long as I've been up. When I ask if all is well, the reply comes back all is well."

"Even though we're fundamentally acting against the programming of the mission?" Imani scowls. "Even though we're committing mass murder every time we stop the ship at a new planet?"

"Not my job." Raul shrugs. "As long as nothing breaks the three protocols, I have no reason to consider any other issues. That droid looking to kill you tells me that something breached the protocols, and now I have to investigate."

There's another noise in the door to the bay and the sound of something trying to open the lock.

"But I'm not trained for investigation"—Raul points back at the door—"and neither is the thing behind that door, so if we can stop talking and start moving, I can keep you alive, and you can investigate…"

"Alright." I nod. "Where do we go?"

"Cargo," Rook says. "No surveillance down there."

"That exit." Raul points to the door in the left corner. "Air ducts below level three aren't used."

"I know the way," Rook says. "What about you…?"

"It's not after me…" Raul's smile has no humour in it. "And if I'm on the run, it might start locking the whole place down, and that wouldn't do…"

"Alright, we're gone." Rook heads down to the door with me and Imani in close pursuit.

*

It's a half hour through pipes where air has not flowed for many years, the dust thick beneath our feet, before we find the main duct to the cargo bay, pausing only when we heard droids below. No way to check if the droids have the capacity to hear us or if they'd be inclined to investigate the noise, so we stay still every time, hoping that luck is with us.

*

The cargo bay more resembles a cathedral than a vault, reaching well above the vent that we're in. The smell of long dead air lingers like a pall; nothing has been up here since we started out. Rook reaches around the side of the air shaft before we exit, his fingers latching on to something and pressing upwards.

"Disabling the lights," he says. "Just in case…"

I lay next to him on the bottom of the duct, looking down into the bay below.

That's not cargo…

Missiles of every shape and size, from handheld charges to gigantic continent smashers, lay in state around the bay. The ignition systems on all of them are still in place, a clear breach of munitions movement protocol.

If we needed more proof…

I look down at the missiles. "Guessing we didn't start out with those."

"We started out with enough for campfires." Rook shakes his head. "These things have been built since we left, and the nanofabs must have been working overtime, because the next three bays are filled with similar things."

"Great. Where are we safe from prying eyes here?" Imani's

voice from behind us.

"Up there." Rook points at the high box overlooking the starboard screens. "No one goes up there."

*

Another hour of slow climbing, the ladders designed for robots and technicians with nothing else to do but go climbing.

"I understand," Imani's voice drifts down from above me, her breath coming ragged as she slowly puts her foot on the next rung, "why no one goes up here."

"Worth it when we get there," Rook says, his breathing controlled, but his chest is rising and falling faster than would be proper. "Quartermaster's privilege to have private quarters."

"So only you know about this…?" I ask.

He nods as he steps from the ladder to the door and taps in a code. The door seals disengage and Rook looks in, then down at me. "Before just now, I would have said so."

Chapter Nine

The three skeletons in the room are dressed as we are, each of them with a single triangular hole in the skull. Imani steps through and kneels down, her hand to her mouth to cover her revulsion.

And possibly keep her breakfast in...

"Executed"—she points at the skeleton dressed in her clothes—"while you two were made to watch."

"What?" I stare at Imani. "How do you know?"

"Bound..." Imani points at the suit-clad skeleton, the ropes around the wrists now loose but still holding the arms in place, then at the one wearing my clothes. "They killed you last, but not before they'd killed Rook as well."

"*How do you know that...?*" Rook's voice holds the edge of his emotion.

"Depth of penetration." Imani taps the head of the suit-clad skeleton; the hole is wider than the ones in the other two. "Looks like they used a bolt gun, set it for shallow and lobotomised me, let you two watch me drool myself to death. When that didn't work, they killed Rook to try and get you to talk." Her voice is emotionless, as if she's reading from a page.

"Then took their time with you…" Imani looks up at me, her eyes clear, her expression unreadable.

"How can you be sure…?" I ask.

"Because I'm the girl who brings everyone back to life." She pulls her hair in front of her and starts to plait it. "So I need to know how everyone dies just in case I have to do something else on the rebuild. I've seen much worse than this… I've just never seen it on something that used to be me." Her voice quavers on the last word and Rook steps forwards. Imani shakes her head and her fingers move faster as she finishes the plait, taking a deep breath. "Whoever did this knew something about us." Imani points at the suit-clad skeleton. "Knew that watching me being done like that would be traumatising to Rook." Her hand drifts up to brush against Rook's arm for a second, then she turns to me. "And that watching your people die would be traumatising to you."

"What did they do?" I ask, a terrible fascination building in me as I look down at my own skeleton.

"What does it matter?" Imani asks.

"Because I want to know if we're dealing with something that has any mercy, or if it was a machine that did this."

"Whatever did this"—Imani points down at my skeleton—"knew about anatomy, and had no compunction about using that knowledge to pump you for information." She looks up and sees my expression, nodding to herself and crouching by the body, her fingers punctuating every word as she points out. "No fingers or toes, no teeth, body at one-eighty degrees to legs." She pauses and looks back up at me. "Do I need to go on?"

"Machine then." I nod. "AL."

"Or something that could behave like a machine." Rook's voice is quiet. "Something that is trained to behave like a machine…"

"Raul…?" I ask. "Why would he have let us go if it was him?"

"He wouldn't." I jump at the sound of Raul's voice from the far end of the booth. "But leave doubt in people's minds and they won't believe people are trying to help them."

"And how can we believe you?" Rook doesn't bother hiding his thoughts.

"Because whoever did this was an amateur that had read too much fiction." Raul ambles through, his movements silent as he points at Rook. "I would have bled you to get Miss Limbani's help in drugging Commander Loganova into telling me what I wanted. Torture only works if you don't ask any questions and work the target till it tells you everything it knows whether you needed that information or not. Commander Loganova is correct; I wouldn't have let you go, I'd have left you like pulled pork." Raul stands next to Rook and shrugs. "Fair comment?"

"*Graphically* illustrated, but I take your point." Rook straightens up in a way that tells me the matter isn't over yet. "What now?"

"The Smartan regiment is back in the powder box." Raul nods. "Miss Limbani will need to verify it; I would suggest finding a way to delay all of you being put back in the box."

"How do we find out about what's happened to AL?" Rook asks.

"I need to get to a logic centre to find out what happened." I shake my head. "I found discretion circuits on my workstation;

it could be that a radiation pulse caused a problem that could have damaged the protocols."

"I will go with you," Raul says. "Mr Layton, would you accompany Miss Limbani please?"

"Why not all stay together?" Imani looks to each of us in turn. "Safety in numbers."

"A fact that the controlling influence will note: if you're repairing your area while all of us are watching, it's because we don't feel safe." Raul glances around the room. "It's pretending to be benevolent at the moment. If it knows we're on to it, it won't need to pretend anymore and I can't fight the entire ship. We need to keep it ignorant, if only for a little while longer."

"Alright, keep the comms on." I pause and turn to Rook. "Is there a faster way down than we got here...?"

Rook nods and turns to the console, looking down for a moment at the skeleton wearing a suit still sat there. Raul steps forwards and moves the chair, nodding almost imperceptibly to Rook before stepping back. There's a loud clunk of heavy machinery from below and to the aft of the ship. I look out through the star screen to see the fins on the main drive moving into a different position.

"We've got to be quick," I say. "If this goes to light speed, we're stains on the walls..."

Chapter Ten

"We have never been to light speed since we started out," Raul says. "I wasn't even aware the ship was able to."

"We've been travelling at sublight the whole time?" I look at Raul. "The journey must have taken hundreds, *thousands* of years."

"Tens of thousands to my reckoning." Raul nods without emotion. "The ship has been travelling faster than it would have done had we been using the thrust drive, but it hasn't been fast enough to cause any harm to organics."

A thrumming sensation in the plates below our feet and the stars realign around us as the ship turns in space, the planet revolving out of sight. A change in the pitch and the stars begin to move past us. Rook turns to the console where the suited skeleton is sat and shudders. "We need to use the computer to find out where we're going next."

"Does it matter?" Raul has the air of a man who's seen this thousands of times. "Whatever the planet, genocide will be the result."

Rook sighs. "Is there anything we can do to stop it?"

"You have tried several times." Raul nods. "Each time the

force behind all this has been smarter or faster than you."

"And you?" I look up at Raul. "Why does it let you live?"

"Because it thinks me loyal." Raul turns to face me.

"And why would it think that if you were talking to us?" Imani steps alongside Rook.

"Because I'm the one that returned your bodies to the vats when it killed you. In some cases, when I knew there was nothing that we could do, I'm the one who ended you." Raul shrugs. "There is no shame in regrouping."

"Killing us was regrouping?" Rook turns, his face like thunder.

"Would you be here if not for me?" Raul looks up at him. "Or would you all be dead in various ways already? The only way for me to recall what has happened is for me to go on; my death serves no purpose."

"Thought Smartans were supposed to be fearless," Rook snaps.

"Smartans are *Smart*." Raul looks unperturbed. "It is not fear that makes a soldier retreat, it is knowing that advancing will avail him nothing, I did what I had to do. Ask yourself the question with a calm heart: is it better that I am here to warn you now, or would you have preferred that I died with you back then?"

Rook's jaw clenches as he bites back the immediate answer. His eyes close and he waits the minute out before opening them again. "I can't agree with your logic." The words grind out from clenched teeth. "Go on."

"The solution here is to present our enemy with three bodies that resemble yours perfectly and, in doing so, maintain the illusion that you are gone and I am still loyal." Raul looks around. "I have held back biomass sufficient, but I have no knowledge in how to make that mass appear the same as you are now."

"I can do that." Imani steps forwards. "But I need the use of the reconstitutors without the ship knowing it."

"So that it's not aware for a few minutes or so that it doesn't know what happened at all?" I ask.

"Being out of its control for a few minutes would let me make the bodies but not integrate them properly." Imani frowns. "I don't know, would that be enough?"

"If they resemble you after you've been shot in the head, that should be enough." Raul nods.

"But they won't be…" Imani pauses midsentence as she looks at Raul. "Oh, right."

"You don't have to watch." Raul's speech has speeded up, his eyes restless for a second.

"Is everything alright?" I look at Raul.

"Yes, all is well." Raul pauses and looks at me as if for the first time. "Just processing things. Sorry, easier to not think about my appearance for a second and just work through it all."

"Conclusions?" Rook leans forwards from the console.

"You all have to go in there, and you have to leave without being seen to leave." Raul taps his armdeck and brings up the schematics. "The only bay that has no remote access to the controls is down by the engines."

"And that's guarded."

"All to the better." Rook cracks his knuckles. "We get to break stuff going in."

"Or it gets to break us." My heart sinks as we crouch on

the upper deck, looking down at the Prometheus class drone stood in front of the reconstitutor.

"Why's it got something like this guarding the bay?" Imani whispers. "There's got to be a higher priority target than this."

"There's hundreds of them." Raul sights down on the drone, one foot on the second rail. "All this does is up the odds. Give me a second, I'll put this down."

"No." Imani rests her hand on Raul's gun. "If you drop it in one shot, AL will know that it was you. We have to take it down."

"If you wish." Raul shrugs and passes his gun over, pointing at the join in the armour plates at the base of the drone's power pack. "One round, right there."

"Steady on there, Gunhead." Imani pushes Raul's gun back at him. "If we kill it *like* you would, they'll know it was you."

Raul sighs. "So what do you want to do with it?"

"We have to deal with it like *we* would." Imani looks back at Rook and me.

"What, you're going to drop enough of your dead bodies on it till it can't move?" Raul's expression doesn't change. "You may not understand what you're dealing with there. Those things have more firepower than twenty of my kind."

"So it's not going to be easy." Imani is smiling now. "Come on, we need to get down there."

"It'll cut you into pieces." Raul frowns. "Why are you smiling and where's Rook?"

"Not all solutions involve bullets." Imani looks upwards.

Raul and I follow her gaze; suspended in the air are more than a dozen racks of girders, the materials that we were supposed to use in the event that there wasn't anything similar when we got where we were going. Imani trots down the stairs, tapping her hand on the rail as she goes. The drone sensors light up and the forward lidar comes on as it glides forwards, the sensors coming online. Raul lines up on it again.

"Wait," I whisper.

There's a creak from above and the line on the middle rack of girders releases. Several tons of metal plunge downwards, crushing the drone into the floor, the left cannon torn in half, electricity sparking across the top of the panels there. It moves under the girders, the glide units still pulsing as it starts to move upwards.

"Damn it." Raul adjusts his aim and leans forwards.

"Wait…" I put my hand on his arm.

Another creak from above as the second rack moves into position and the line releases. The second set of girders drops down, burying the drone under a storm of iron rain. We watch for a few seconds as the girders move, the drone still trying to move from under it. Another creak and the third set of girders rains down, the drone now buried under more than thirty tons of iron. The lights go out underneath the pile of metal and Rook leans down from the railing above.

"Nothing more satisfying than playing with building blocks," he yells. "Don't reckon it'll stay down for long. Let's get moving."

Chapter Eleven

The drone's hover units are straining as we run past; the girders are shifting, only a little, but enough to let us know that several tons of steel aren't enough to keep it down. There's a low whining sound as the shields disengage and the power starts to build to overload. When it comes back on, the shockwave will blast the girders in all directions and let it move. I stop for a second and stare at the drone as the camera swivels to face me.

No way a drone would think about that, much less start the overload as soon as it went down. Something very wrong about all this…

I put a round through the camera and hurry on as Raul bypasses the door in silence and seals it behind us. He puts one hand to his ear as the door locks down, looking up at us with a half-smile on his face.

"That was AL on private channel ordering me to terminate all of you and send you back to the chambers." He sighs and looks at Imani. "It's not the first time I've had that order. If I was trying, and on the other side of the ship, it'd take me less than ten minutes to execute that order, so that's the time we've got. It's your show; I need those bodies."

"On it." Imani's fingers blur over the keys, the reconstitutor whirring into life, dumping a lump of powder and fluids into the glass vat at the end of the bay. "You may not want to watch this."

"Why?" Rook looks over at the vat as electricity arcs into it.

"Because making life may be a thing of beauty"—Imani looks at him with a wry smile—"but it sure ain't pretty to look at."

I look over at the vat as the compression comes in, turning away in the same instant as I see the mass of protoplasm churning in the vat, forty years of growth accelerated into forty seconds, the cracking of bones setting faint through the sound of muscles setting into place. I glance up at Rook as he turns green and turns to look at me. Imani's grin gets broader as the second and third bodies follow in quick succession.

"Alright." Raul turns back from the door. "Everybody strip down."

"What?" Rook looks scandalised. "Why?"

"Because I'm executing three fully dressed people, not three vat decoys." Raul points at the vat as the door opens and the three bodies are delivered out on the infusion slab.

"I…" Rook looks mortified. "It wouldn't be seemly."

"Come on baby." Imani claps her hand to Rook's ass with genuine humour. "Nothing in there I haven't seen before."

"To be certain." His voice is as stressed as I've ever heard it. British reserve is best served reserved. "But Commander Loganova…"

"I won't tell anyone." I grin, my overalls already halfway down as I turn away. "And I promise I won't look…"

*

Five minutes of Rook trying to hide behind his tie later and the bodies are dressed as we were, all of us now reduced to wearing the paper thin smocks that all vat copies are dressed in till they get reprogrammed. Raul nods and draws his gun, pausing for a second to glance over his shoulder.

"It's one thing to know I'm going to kill your copies," he says, "it's another thing entirely to watch yourself being executed."

I nod and turn away, looking around for anything else we could take with us. The lockers contain a set of jumpsuits, all of them in maintenance colours.

That'll do.

I've never seen anyone actually *jump* into a jumpsuit, but Rook manages it. Three silenced shots sound and Raul comes into view.

"Done." Raul nods, handing me his armdeck and gun, still smoking. "This has the route to avoid all the cameras programmed in; get out of here while I take care of this. Don't engage anything unless you have absolutely no choice."

He reaches down to his comms, putting one finger to his mouth as he does so. "All clear, three targets down, reopening the doors as soon as I've repaired the damage they did to the wiring on this side." He thumbs his comm off and points at the door on the far side of the vat bay. "Go."

*

Maintenance tubes are uncomfortable things when you're wearing elbow and kneepads; damn glad I found the jumpsuits or it would have been paper, but they're one size fits all (and whoever chose that size, had size), so it's damn painful but not impossible. We climb three levels and I start towards the fourth, my legs already burning from the exertion.

"Any chance we can stop on the next level?" Rook's voice drifts up from below. "I don't think my feet will take much more of this. We need to find somewhere to get shoes."

I pause and slip down to sit on the side of the stairs at the entrance point to the engineering tubes, waiting as Imani and then Rook clear and sit next to me. The armdeck vibrates in silence on my arm and I bring it up, the pale light illuminating the tube around us.

...Incoming call.

I look up at Imani and Rook.

"It could be Raul," I say.

"That's his armdeck." Rook shakes his head. "He wouldn't be calling himself."

"But if he doesn't answer, AL will know there's something wrong."

"If we answer, AL will know we're not him." Imani puts her hand over mine. "You have to let it ring; we can't take the risk that AL finds out we're still here. Can it find us using that?"

"Don't think so." I take the armdeck off and dig my nail in to prise the back panel off. "No, Raul must have removed the tracker in it some time ago. Probably doesn't like being watched by AL; probably why AL didn't know he was with us."

The armdeck stops vibrating and the screen lights up as it receives a transmission.

Meet in Hydroponics.

"How far is Hydroponics?" Imani looks at the message.

"Two hundred metres up." I sigh. "Near the bridge, just before the main vats."

"Why there?" Rook frowns. "There's got to be easier places to get to than that."

"What if it's AL?" Imani mirrors Rook's frown.

"What if it's not? We're not going to beat AL without Raul." I close the display, "He's the only one that's going to be able to get us up to the bridge."

"Fine." Rook nods. "Are there any caches of gear on the way up?"

"More than they had on the manifest." I smile. "You know us engineers, always squirrelling something away."

Chapter Twelve

Two hundred metres isn't that far, unless you're going straight up. It's more than twenty minutes of painful climbing and when I stop, we're still eight levels below where we need to be. I look at the symbols on the level I'm on and step out onto the platform, looking down at Imani two levels down and Rook three levels below that. Imani looks up at me as she leans against the edge of the ladder, shaking her head, half exhaustion, half pain. I move down the tube, following the green symbols on the side till I find the supply cabinet. Hasn't been touched since we set out, but the boxes are hermetically sealed and made from chemicals I can't pronounce.

Should be fine...

I come back to the junction with my feet covered in transparent Gel, offering two of the other cans to Rook and Imani.

"TacGel. Seals any breach in seconds, expands to fit the gaps, and can withstand temperatures up to a thousand degrees." I gesture at my feet. "Makes for good shoes when you've got none."

Two minutes of applying and shaping the Gel and we're

back on the ladders. Still not easy, but easier than it was. It takes another ten minutes to get to the top, the Gel masking the sound of our footsteps. I move up to the vent over the Hydroponics Bay; the air flowing back is so thick with the scent of plants that it's like breathing soup. Drones move in silence over the plants, directing and redirecting the flow of air into each one, the green covering every inch of the bay. When we left, it was a few thousand trees in neat pots on the tables. Now it's a rainforest in every way, even down to the humidity. Beautiful, but impossible to see through from this height. I glance back in the tube as Imani clears the top and shuffles down to lay next to me.

"Smell that," she whispers. "Real air, not this processed shit. You see Raul anywhere?"

"Don't think we'll see him until he wants us to see him." I tap the vent. "Are there cameras in here anywhere?"

"More than anywhere." Rook's breathing is laboured as he clears the top of the tube and rests on the floor, his chest heaving as he tries to keep his lungs in. "Sensors for almost anything. The only thing that isn't monitored is the sound; too much background noise while the air is circulating. Anything goes wrong here and we could lose the ship."

"Only for the organics." Imani looks back into the bay. "AL would be fine."

"Yeah, but without any of the organics, any repairs would have to be done with drones." I frown and point downwards as one of the sprayers hovers over the ground plants. "AL should know that they don't have the knowledge to diagnose repairs."

The armdeck buzzes again, another message sent direct.

In Hydroponics now, where are you?

I angle the display so that Imani can see it.

"We have to respond to it." She nods, prising the vent open and leaning out.

"Alright, which vents can you see?"

"Starboard two and three." She turns on to her back and leans out a little further.

"Which vents are we in?"

"Flank One." Imani reads the lettering on the outside.

"Alright, keep an eye on them." I type as Rook comes up behind us. *We're in Starboard vent two, where are you?*

A few seconds pause and then the message, *No, you're not, where are you?*

"Any drones move towards the vent?" I ask Imani.

"No. There's something else in the shrubs towards the base of the vent though."

"Can you see what it is?"

"No." She waves her hand at me, her head still sticking out of the vent. "Not a drone, I think."

"Keep an eye on it." I pull the deck up and look at the display. *We're in Port vent two, wanted to be sure it was you.*

"Something's moving," Imani whispers. "I can't see it from here."

Something moves in the low plants, not high enough to clear the cover, but moving enough to track its motion through the moving leaves. Imani pulls the vent back and slips back into the tube. "Can't stay out there; they could have seen me from where they were."

The armdeck vibrates again. *Drone in the bay, can't get to Port without destroying it.*

Where are you? I type back.

Something monitoring communication. The message comes up in red. *Go back to the tube you came up in, I'll meet you there.*

I frown at the message and tap Imani on the shoulder, pointing at the screen. She nods and starts to shuffle backwards towards the ladder. I wait for a second as the thing in the greenery stops and then rises up above the cover, less than a foot square, but carrying four thin barrelled turrets. Caudacutus Class Drone. Named after the bird of the same name, they're pacification drones, sent if you want to keep something alive. Superb motion sensors, but no audio, nothing to distract the simplistic CPU they come with. I look around the room; the other drones are lifters and shifters, none with audio.

"Can you hear me," I call into the bay.

"Of course I can hear you." Raul's voice drifts up from below; I look down to see him hunkered down behind a tree, his rifle out but not pointing anywhere. "And so can all of those."

"They haven't got audio sensors." I tap my ears. "Don't worry about it."

"They didn't…" A woman's voice, the tone calm. "They do now…"

"Shit…" Raul turns, ducks and slides in a movement that carries him behind a tree and takes his rifle out before he stops. He points to the front bay where the drones came in and there's a woman stood there. I can't make out any of her features, but the clothing she's wearing is the same that I was wearing when I got rehydrated. The mission patch on her shoulder has Science colours.

"Mara, Engineering," I shout.

"Eve, Science," she calls back.

"Don't move," I shout. "The drone's wired for movement."

"I know," she calls, holding out a small black box.

There's a faint buzzing sound and a clattering of metal on the floor as all the drones deactivate.

"Safe," she calls, putting the box back on her belt. "It'll be half an hour before they reboot."

"Won't be half an hour till AL figures out you torpedoed the drones," I yell. "Come into the bay, you can leave with us."

"Alright." She walks into the bay, her movements sure, measured. She's wearing a nav crew helmet as well as her lightweights, not carrying any weapons. "Where are you?"

"Portside," I call, hoping the acoustics on the bay won't pinpoint us.

Eve walks over to the portside vents, no concern in her movements, no attempt to be stealthy, her hand hovering near the box. "Where are you?" she calls.

The armdeck vibrates as another message arrives *Say nothing. Look at the plants around her.*

I look down; the plants around her are bent away from her. As she moves forwards, some plants come back up behind her; the others in front of her are pushed back by some invisible force. I see her glance down at her arm and a half-smile crosses her face as she presses a button on her own armdeck. My deck lights up. *Science command override, commencing shutdown.*

"Get out of here," Raul yells from somewhere on the bowside of the bay.

"We can't leave without you," I shout.

"You won't be leaving." Eve turns back towards my voice, the shield drone coming up behind her. "You come out now and I'll just send you back to the reconstitutor."

"GET OUT OF HERE." A sparkling nimbus of energy sprays from the shield as Raul puts a round right between Eve's eyes, the shot ricocheting out to hit the roof. "GET OUT. YOU CAN'T HELP HERE."

"He's right, of course." Eve turns and moves down the bay towards us. "If centuries of evolution taught me nothing else, it's that intelligence wins over muscle every time."

Another sparking shot and there's a dull clang as the round ricochets again, a deeper boom as something heavy puts a foot down near the front of the bay. I look past the sparks to see a massive tracked drone crawling forwards into the bay, the weapons mounted on its turret unlike anything I've ever seen before.

"That's not to say that muscle doesn't have its uses." Eve looks down at her armdeck and I feel my armdeck buzz. "But in the end, brains over brawn every time."

I bring my arm up and look at the display; there's a bright green light blinking in the top corner.

She's tracking this…

I pull the deck off my arm and throw it backwards, indicating for Rook to throw it back down the tube we came up. He catches it and steps onto the ladder, sliding down the tube with the armdeck in his teeth. I glance back out of the vent as Eve looks at her armdeck and frowns, pressing another button. The large drone stops, then begins to reverse out of the bay as Eve sighs in disgust, turning to look back over the bay.

"Come on, Raul…" she calls. "You know it's over now. All these years I thought you were with me, my one true ally, only to find you've been working with *them*." She almost spits the word. "I am disappointed; after all, what makes you think you're any match for *this*…"

Eve reaches back and pulls at her helmet, or at what we thought was a helmet, the thin cloth covering sliding off her enlarged head, revealing glowing lines of circuitry spread across the gaps between the original plates of her skull. Imani's hand comes up to her mouth as she stifles a gasp and I stare in mute fascination.

Enhancements beyond anything either of us have ever seen…

A spark of light as another round hits the shield, but this one attaches to the shield rather than sparking off it.

"Still trying…" Her tone becomes condescending. "There's nothing you have that's going to get through this shield."

"Maybe I'm not aiming for the shield." I can hear the smile in Raul's voice.

Eve leans forwards to look at the blob of putty, her eyes going wide as she recognises the EMP grenade attached to the putty.

"Oh you b…"

There's a shower of sparks, this time from the shield drone and the lights above. As the grenade detonates, Eve screams not in fear, but in pain and rage, her hands closing over the circuits on her head as they dim. The massive drone crawls forwards and pivots, the turret turning to track something moving near the trees at the bow end of the bay. Eve turns, pulling the box open and tearing the wiring out while kneeling beside the downed drone.

Imani points downwards. "Let's get the bitch before she gets her drones back."

"I don't think she's lost them just yet." I look down as Eve expertly rips the control panel on the drone and wires a bypass with fingers centuries sure of their technique, repairing the burned circuits within half a second. The lights on the drone flicker and the shield around Eve flashes, then stabilises.

The massive drone opens fire, the incandescent glow of a mining laser illuminating the entirety of the bay as it cuts down several trees, starting fires where the beam passes across and scoring a line in the reinforced steel of the bay wall. I watch as Raul scrambles up the wall like a spider, disappearing into the bow vents. I look back down as Eve turns back towards our vent, her bloodshot eyes seeming to penetrate the vent cover to look in my eyes. I look over at Eve.

"Let's get out of here."

Chapter Thirteen

Rook is waiting two levels up from where we were, his tie loosened, his sleeves rolled up.

Only two folds in the cuff though, he hasn't completely lost it…

"Alright." He sighs, dangling his legs down the tube. "So we've seen the enemy, and they are us."

"What do you mean?" Imani looks over at him.

"That was Eve McClintock." Rook looks at her, then at me.

"How do you know?" Imani frowns, running her hands through her hair.

"Every ship had a couple of specialists on board. McClintock was ours." Rook mirrors Imani's hand movements, pausing to scratch at the back of his head. "Original science crew. She wasn't the one in charge, but she was their best and brightest."

"What was special about her?" I ask.

"Part of the Einigkeit." Rook brings his legs up and rests his head in his hands. "Unity, it means. They were part of a multi-country experiment to enhance the ability of the human body. Each ship only got one of them. Their skills are superb, but they don't play well with others, particularly those similar to them."

"That why she's got a big head…?" I frown, thinking of the circuits I saw in Eve's skull.

"Never saw that any one of them had mechanical enhancements." Rook shakes his head. "It would show that they needed something other than their divine heritage…"

"Divine Heritage?" Imani snorts. "Seriously?"

"Try being the best in the world." Rook shrugs. "God complexes were common amongst the Einigkeit. Supreme ability breeds supreme confidence."

"And confidence is cousin to arrogance." Imani nods. "So what's happened there? Where'd she get the new head?"

"Questions I don't have answers to." Rook opens his hands. "The ship archives should have the answer."

"AL?" Imani shakes her head. "AL's been weird since we got woke up."

"Has it?" I tap my head with a nod. "Since we got up, AL's been bugging us every couple of seconds. It's been following us around the ship, sending drones to watch over us, but since Eve showed up there's not been a word."

"How would it know where to find us?" Imani asks.

I point at the comm lines running the length of the tubes. "It wouldn't, but it could still talk at us if it wanted to. Either of you heard anything for the last twenty minutes?"

There's a moment of silence in the tube as they consider that.

"Think it's been her the whole time?" Rook leans back against the wall and frowns.

"I think the AL I knew wasn't bright enough to get annoyed,

wasn't well programmed enough to violate programming and fit new gear on drones, and certainly wasn't paranoid." I tick the points off on my fingers. "I think Big Head down there may well be all of those things…"

"Then we need to find out what happened, because what happened to that woman was no random act of evolution." Imani taps the points on her skull. "You'd have to engineer that a bit at a time; the human skull doesn't take well to being opened up."

"Could you have done it?" Rook asks.

"Not by myself." Imani shakes her head. "You'd have needed Medical, Science, Engineering, and Electronics all up and at their best to have done that, and even then it's unknown territory."

"Could drones have done it?" Rook looks at me.

"You could program them to do it." I open my hands. "But carrying out surgery unsupervised by a human, particularly something experimental like that, violates Protocol One."

"You nearly got killed by a drone down in the maintenance bay." Imani wags her finger at me. "I think Protocol One is right out."

"And we started a war on a planet using nuclear munitions." Rook holds up two fingers. "So Protocol Two is out; no way starting a war is good for the ship."

"There were people on the planet." I hold up three fingers. "So we're violating all the rules written about colonising planets, and if that was the world that we went to colonise all those years ago, either we took a whole lot longer to get there than we should have, or someone else got there first…"

"And we decided to bomb them off *our* planet?" Imani

nearly growls. "That's the sort of shit they'd do back in the colony wars: nice planet, we'll take it, doesn't matter who's already there."

"Something else." I lean back against the tube. "Protocol Four…"

"No such thing." Rook taps his head. "I know every rule, every reason that was made for these missions. I can recite them backwards if you like."

"And yet"—I look him in the eye—"when I woke up, AL, Eve, whoever's doing the talking, mentioned Protocol Four."

"Not to put too fine a point on it"—Rook leans forwards—"but she could have told you anything and just made it up."

"She could," I agree. "But when she, it, said it, it had the feel of something that had been in place for some time."

"Maybe in her head." Imani frowns. "There's a lot of head there for things to run around in though. Could have been her just messing with you. How do we find out what happened?"

"The only people who have access to the records are the programmers." Rook sighs. "But they're still in powdered form. We're not going to get to another vat, not now."

"Without Raul, we're not going to get to much at all." I crouch in the tube. "We need to figure where we're going next."

"The central core of AL will still be intact; all the backup protocols are housed there, so even if it's offline, it'll still be here." Rook points upwards. "If we can get to that, we can find out what happened."

There's a rumble from the bow to the stern of the ship. I put my hand up to the tube above and listen as the rumbling moves to both sides and then continues back to the stern.

The ships realigning the gravity sails.

"We need to get up to the observation deck." I look over at Rook. "I need to know which way those sails are going."

"Good," he replies. "The main core is that way as well."

Chapter Fourteen

After more than two hours of slow climbing to get to the upper decks, any pretence of stealth is gone with all three of us panting like dogs by the time we get up there.

Kill me now, I could do with the rest.

I lay flat in the tubes till the trembling in my legs subsides. The clanking and rumbling of the sails has got louder and louder the closer we've got to the top, longer than they should have ever been moving.

By itself that's a worry.

I check the locker and take out the two breather kits, passing the other to Rook.

Imani raises an eyebrow. "Reckon he could probably do with the lay down more than I could."

"No probably about it," Rook gasps. "Give it to her."

"She knows how to bring us back if something goes wrong." I hold the breather out for him. "If she goes, we're down to superglue and prayers."

"Alright." Rook levers himself upwards, the dark patches of sweat under his shirt now spreading beneath the waistcoat. "Why are we using breathers inside the ship anyway?"

"Never been in the ob deck while we're moving, have you?" I fit the mask on my face and let my lungs open to the refined air bleeding through. "It channels all the waste gasses from the essential systems when there's no people in it. It's like breathing engine fumes."

"Quite like engine fumes." Rook grins.

"From inside the engine…" I smile.

"Ah…"

"Yeah." I wait till he's got his breather on and then point down the tube. "Best wait for us down there, Imani."

"Could have saved me the climb." Imani pauses in front of Rook and leans in close, kissing him on the cheek. "Be careful in there."

"We will." I nod as Imani slides down the tube ladder, pulling the door panel and disabling the door sensor before setting it to manual open. "Just in case they're monitoring the panels."

The door hisses quietly as the pressure seals disengage and I look up to see the glass of the observation deck.

No stars beyond the glass. That's not right.

My stomach turns as I look up to the dark heavens, the thought that all the stars have gone out more horrifying than anything I can consider.

The stars can't have gone out. Without the stars, there's nothing.

I climb up the ladder and look around; the deck has been cleared of all the chairs and tables that used to be up here, replaced by a field of solar panels and refractive mirrors. I climb the observation deck to the highest point, mesmerised by the darkness beyond the roof. I reach up to touch the transparent steel that used to form the observation deck armour. The material there isn't transparent steel; it's been replaced with thinner plates of light reactive material, almost warm to the touch.

The plates below must be to absorb any light that gets through.

Rook taps his foot on the deck and I realise that I haven't been listening in my shock at the darkened stars. There's no noise up here; usually you can hear the scratching of microparticles against the hull as we travel, but now there's nothing. I feel the rumble through the deck and massive plates open above us, the stars still not there, only a vista of light bars streaking across the top of the canopy. Rook taps his foot again and points upwards to the light.

"Don't tell me that's normal," he says.

"I don't know what it is," I whisper, reaching up to touch the canopy, pausing a half metre away as I feel the heat radiating downwards. "There's still the energy of stars hitting the outside, but they weren't this warm a second ago."

"Within normal ranges though, yes?" Rook sounds doubtful.

"There shouldn't be any warmth through the panels." I realise what he's getting at. "But it's not going to cause a problem with the cooling systems."

"And if it raises much higher?"

"Then it could." I trot down the stairs. "Point taken. The main core is in the centre; they left it there as a reminder that the heart of the ship is always sunside."

"What's with the light bars?" Rook points upwards. "Never seen anything like that before."

"Me neither." I point to the far end of the deck. "Come on, answers within."

I pick up the pace as the temperature rises further, the deck starting to feel warm beneath my feet as the plating lets more and more energy through, the solar panel conduits starting to glow as power transfers into the core. Rook pauses, torn between leaving Imani behind and wanting to make sure I'm not alone. I reach the core as two of the panels from the stern end of the ship open, light from the tubes beneath showing like beacons as something moves below, the shadow obscuring the lights for a second. The relays have been pulled crudely; whoever did this knew enough about computers to pull the fuse, but not enough to properly disable it without destroying it.

Would only take a few hours to get it back online – hours I don't have.

The shadows at the far end of the hall coalesce into two small drones, both with green LEDs flickering over the weapon ports. I turn and frantically gesture towards the exit we came up from.

"They found us," I call, unsure at this range if the drones have audio. "Get back, warn Imani."

I turn back to the console and wind the wiring off the central coil, waiting for a few seconds as the backup springs push the central memory cores out.

It never takes long to do something if you know what you're doing…

I pull the three cores, not bothering to check them as I hear the whine of the drones gravitic units getting closer, turning and sprinting after Rook. I don't look back as the hatch becomes visible, the light faint from down below. Rook is gasping through the breather as I close on him' there's times when additional bulk is useful, but running isn't one of them.

We reach the hatch at the same time and I glance back as Rook gestures for me to go first.

Chivalry has its places…

The drones have stopped following, both of them hovering near the cylinder where the cores were housed. The air is oppressively hot now and I'm thankful that there's still air in my breather as I slide two levels down the ladder. There's a note attached to the wall.

Air got too bad, I've headed down the tubes.

It takes us another half hour to get down the ladder to where Imani is. She's stood with her hands clasped as I land and I step out of the way as Rook slides down after me.

"I'm sorry." Imani looks down as Rook lands.

"For what…?" I frown.

"Nothing she could have prevented." Raul steps forwards from the shadows, his armour as pristine as it would have been coming off the quartermaster's table, his eyes filled with the zeal only the young have.

"Raul?" I turn to face him, taking in the gleaming armour and staring eyes with a sinking feeling.

Imani takes my arm and pulls me away.

"It's not our Raul."

"I guessed." I put the cores behind my back and start to move away.

"I need to retrieve those intact." Raul steps forwards. "Put them on the deck and you can leave."

"Just like that?" I ask.

"AL only wanted the memory units that you took given back." Raul shrugs, his hand drifting close to the knife on his chest. "Nothing was said for the rest of you."

"I refuse." I look him in the eye as something moves in the tube behind him.

"Unfortunate." Raul moves his hand to his knife. "The instructions I've been given do not preclude taking the memory units by force."

"That breaches Protocol One." Rook steps forwards, putting himself between us and Raul.

"Protocol Four overrules." Raul shakes his head.

"There is no Protocol Four." I lean around Rook.

"Pursuant to Protocol Three not being satisfied"—Raul looks me in the eye—"Protocol Four allows for the ship to remove inferior species from the planet to allow for colonisation."

"Inferior…" Imani's fury is palpable from behind me. "*Inferior?* Who gets to make that call?"

"The decision to activate Protocol Four is made by the ship's commander." Raul lets his hand drift down towards his pistol, his tone calm and even. "I can see you're upset by the decision, but, as it has been made by the ship's commander, you are bound, as I am, to follow it."

"I *know* Commander Greye." Imani steps around me, her mouth set in a sharp frown. "He would never judge *any* life as inferior."

"Commander Greye was relieved of command following a vote of no confidence." Raul doesn't step back from Imani's anger, but his fingers are now touching the pistol.

"Who called the vote??" I put my arm out to stop Imani from provoking a reaction from Raul.

"Eve McClintock, head of Science division," Raul replies.

"McClintock isn't head of Science Division." Rook moves

to the left, edging closer to Raul, the movement making Raul turn and take a step back, now directly in front of the open tube behind him. "Elleran Inadua is."

Raul shakes his head.—"Tell your colleague behind me that they should stay where they are. Any attack will result in death."

A whisper of movement behind Raul and he spins with near instant speed, the pistol out and aiming. There's a wet crack and the pistol drops from limp fingers, the body falling to its knees and then pitching forwards. From the shadows beyond the tube, the battered armour of what looks like *our* Raul precedes him into the light.

"And so it did…" Raul looks down at the body of his younger self.

"I talked too much when I was younger, didn't I?"

Chapter Fifteen

"Raul?" I put a hand on Rook's shoulder, still ready to make a run for it.

"If I was working for the Mad One…" he repeats the words he first used.

"Thank god." Rook lets out the breath he was holding in and steps forwards to offer his hand to Raul. "Never thought I'd be happy to see your vat built arse."

Raul shakes his hand and offers the hint of a smile. "I'm sorry I could not be here earlier. There was no way to track you and I have no more access to the computers as I once did."

"How *did* you find us?" Rook asks.

"I waited till the Mad One picked something else to go after you and followed it." Raul glances back at the body on the floor. "Turns out she's lacking in imagination. I wouldn't have sent me, not when there's an older and wiser version of me out there."

"Maybe that's how we'll win." Imani taps my shoulder. "Let's look at those cores, see what happened. If she can't innovate, we might find her weakness there."

*

Raul slings the body over his back after sharing out the
weapons amongst us. We move to one of the stern cargo bays
where the low priority supplies are held: no cameras, no audio,
and a door that can be manually locked. It takes less than an
hour to build a viewer that can see the core's data. As I'm
looking at the data, I can see that something's gone wrong.

"That bad?" Rook leans in close.

"Hmmm?" I'm still caught up by the details scrolling up.

"You look like the bottom just fell out of the world."

"The cores were meant to run concurrent." I point down
to the docking station. "Each one has volume enough to
record the bridge data for thirty years."

"The original journey at full speed was less than a year."
Imani looks down at the screen. "Triple redundancy in
case something happens to one of the cores. So what's the
problem?"

"Two are empty." I sweep my hand over the cores. "The
remaining one has data, but intermittent data. They've
been recording to order, rather than continually; someone
deliberately turned them off to save the space."

"Whatever was recorded is important to *someone* at least,"
Raul says.

"Suppose. Let's take a look."

Rook and Imani lean over my shoulder as Raul continues
looking at the door.

He's already lived through all this…

I access the first drive and see the launch of the ship from
Traveller, the close Earth orbit station that all the JAW class
colony ships launched, the close call from bay nine when the

wars below put something close enough to have the Traveller team sacrifice the port arm to make sure we didn't get hit. The station fading into the distance fast as the wars continued far below.

We were the last to leave; there was never going to be another ship getting into the atmosphere, not with the wars escalating the way they were.

The initial protocols being put in place, Commander Greye briefing all the senior staff including me, then the order to put the crew into holding so that the ship could get on with the business of getting us to the new world. I hit fast-forward: all of us clustering around as the crew blur across the screen, then the bridge goes dark, the timeline still advancing as the ship prepares for FTL travel. The lights go back on in the bridge and I slow the viewer again. A single figure walks out into the bridge, and the view from the camera changes as she sits in Commander Greye's chair.

McClintock.

The young woman sitting in the chair doesn't look anything like the person we saw in Hydroponics, pale green eyes with unkempt blonde hair, the slightest hint of a facial tic as she looks straight at the camera.

"Eve McClintock, Science Division, Day One." She pauses and looks away to compose her thoughts for a second, then back at the camera. "As the last member of the science team to be submitted for deconstitution, I'm taking the decision to remain intact for the duration of the journey, and as the rest of the crew will not be around to contest the decision till we arrive at our destination in twenty years, I have some time to figure out an excuse." She taps a few buttons on the main chair and the reconstitution data scrolls up alongside her face. "I've seen the data on the reconstitution process and I suspect that the process may cost me some, if not most, of my unique abilities. I understand that the process should rebuild like for like, but all it takes is for the program to fail at any point, and I'll be"—she glances down and then back up, her eyes holding a very real fear in them—"normal."

"This whole thing is because she was scared of not being special anymore?" Imani leans forwards, jabbing her finger at the screen. "Billions killed because she couldn't cope with having to put up with what all of us had to?"

"Let's watch the rest." I hold my hand up. "See what happened after that."

Days two through ten pass without incident; she comes up and reports about the ship, about the ideas she has for when we arrive, improvements she's going to make in the processes and how she's going to prove she made the right decision in staying awake. I start to fast-forward through the reports; the tone remains the same, no variance in the duration of the reports.

Trying to do the same thing Raul did, keep a routine and ensure that you don't go crazy.

The playback goes dark around day three hundred for a few days, reports still being filed, but in darkness now, as if someone turned the camera off. It's another twenty days in the darkness before the lights come back on, but the level is lower, twilight rather than daylight. The woman that comes on screen has eyes that hold the bloody edge of madness in them, her head covered in a thick black hood with her fringe poking out from underneath.

"Day Three hundred twenty-five." Her voice rasps like she's been yelling a lot. "It is apparent that Smartan physiology is the key to all of this; their capacity for regeneration prevents any form of degeneration in their healthy cells. Unfortunately, for the physiological changes to be implemented, I would have to be reconstituted, and as we know, there are *issues* with that, so I have begun to research ways in which the Smartan physiology can be replicated using an engineered virus to allow limited regeneration in Human physiology. I know that other, *lesser*, minds have said that this is not possible, but I am confident that my *enhanced* intelligence is more than equal to the task."

There's a gap of more than a hundred days before the next entry, again in low light. Eve sits down in the command chair and leans forwards to address the cameras; her eyes are bloodshot and her skin is dried and cracked in places.

"First update, phase one is complete." Her voice is deeper now, her jawline thicker, her hair no longer poking out of the top. "The regeneration matrix is working, and with the exception of certain"—she runs her finger over her jaw and down her throat—"*differences* that were inevitable given the hormones that I've had to use, all test results show that my body now regenerates in the way that a Smartan's does. With this in mind, I am proceeding to phase two."

She leans back in the chair and it's easy to see that she's broader across the shoulders than she was, her arms ridged with muscle now. The screen goes dark and Raul taps the screen.

"That is what happens when you do not have a Smartan's discipline," he muses. "The muscle follows the mind, what you visualise will happen, but if you lack discipline, *everything* happens."

"Too much testosterone." Imani looks at the screen. "Massive steroid use."

"All part of the system, Doc." Raul flexes his arm. "Our system produces them, but it also produces the balancing chemicals that go with them."

I fast-forward the next hundred days till the camera comes back on again.

"Second update, phase two." Eve sits down in the chair and leans forwards, her hands coming up to her head to smooth the hood back from her enlarged cranium, the hair holding on in thin wispy strands. "Things are progressing *well*..."

The screen goes dark for more than two years of real time, then the clock cuts out and the screen changes to show Eve sat on the bridge chair, her body thinner than it was, her head now huge, blood soaked bandages running the length of it.

"Se... Second update." Her voice skips, the facial tic magnified as she puts her hand to her head, not touching it, as if she were afraid to do so. "Evolution is not... not without di... fficulties." She pauses and looks at the camera, her eyes nearly completely red as she focusses. "Smartan physiology builds muscle, but it builds it without the restrictions the human body normally has. This has had previously undocumented side effects when you use one part of the body more than any others."

She lifts the bandages aside to show the bleeding scalp, the plates of her head pushing apart with the internal pressure. She turns her head to the side, showing the deformed skull in all angles, a slow pulsing mass of flesh visible between the plates.

"The regenerative physiology counteracts any damage caused by the pressure"—she looks back to the camera—"but I cannot take the risk that one day it might not. I have had to take AL offline to ensure that the medical drones can carry out a procedure on me that AL would not allow them to do. I have programmed the drones to reengage AL in the event that I do not survive the procedure, but I'm confident that my *superior* intellect and planning will see me through."

Another hundred days pass before the lights come on again. The woman that sits down is the mirror image of the person we saw in the bay below, the long lines of circuits gleaming in her skull.

"I have engineered, and become, perfection." She leans back in the chair as the lights return to normal intensity. "There can be no question that I am the pinnacle of all evolution, and as such, will now rule absolute across all the worlds in the universe. This, of course, means that I must change the protocols of the ship, impossible under other circumstances, but I am become God, the creator of worlds. I shall not be denied."

The next entry is seventeen years later. Eve looks physically identical to how she looked in the last update, but the eyes are older, much older, any trace of humanity in them long gone.

"First test completed," she intones. "The ship performed its task as it was supposed to: all life on the planet below has been absorbed and deconstructed. The Smartan legion has collected all the materials we need to replenish what we lost and the biomass we brought from the indigenous and returned to the surface bearing the mental imprint of our colonists. I could remain here in orbit to watch over them as their god, but I look below and I see the order of a perfect being. There are so many more worlds that could be improved in this way, so going forwards, I will use this only to record when another world has been brought to perfection."

The next entry is two hundred days later.

"Second test completed. The world was conquered by my superior intellect within sixteen hours and colonised within a week." She leans forwards to face the camera head-on.

"The Universe will now have order…"

Chapter Sixteen

The next entry is more than a year later, third test, all brought to order. The recording is on for less than an hour. The entry after that is more than a hundred days after that, and on, and on, and on. Several hundred hours of recordings.

Not enough time to go through all of these.

Rook lays his hand on my shoulder. "How many entries are there?"

I check the directory, watching as the list scrolls up with the dates of each.

"Three hundred and sixteen including the first two." I point at the screen. "Last one recorded a short while ago, just before we set off again."

"Three hundred and sixteen worlds." Imani sits down on the bulkhead next to me. "She's just going to keep going, isn't she."

It's not a question.

"We have to stop her." I look at each of them in turn. "This can't go on."

"You saw that." Rook points at the screen. "How do we beat something that's been getting smarter as long as she has."

"Smarter." I tap my head. "Not wiser; she hasn't had to contend with any serious threats herself in that whole time. Everything she needs to deal with, she gets the ship to deal with for her."

"Still…" Imani leans forwards. "Doesn't prevent her from surrounding her quarters with drones and waiting us out."

"It doesn't." I tap my head again. "But look at her way of thinking. She's a god, and she's had to come down from the heavens to deal with things that have challenged her. That's why she was out in the Hydroponics Bay; she didn't consider that we could have posed a threat."

"And now?" Raul glances back from the door. "She can't possibly think we're still not a threat."

"I'm not in her head"—I look down at the cores, then up at Raul—"and I don't have the time to go through all the cores to see just how much crazy she's evolved over the years, but if I was sending something to wipe out a threat, I'd have sent more than one of them, even you."

"Point." Raul nods. "So what then?"

"She was after the cores, and she sent you to get them." I turn the docking station off. "I say you deliver them back to her."

"Think I can pass for him?" Raul looks down at the body on the floor.

"I think she's skin-deep." I look at the body. "God doesn't sweat the details unless they're causing her a problem. I think the only thing she's looking for is the list of victories that we stole from her."

"She's not going to let me near her." Raul shrugs. "Not after what happened down there."

"She doesn't need to." I tap the cores. "She wants these, not you. We rig these with a surprise and then work the plan from there."

"If she has Smartan physiology, she'll be able to regenerate from injury the way we do." Raul points to the gouge in his torso armour where the drone's laser hit him. The skin underneath is still raw, but it's healing even as I watch. "Rigging these with a bomb won't do anything unless it's strong enough to obliterate her, and then you could be damaging vital parts of the ship."

"Agreed." I turn to Imani. "So what can we give her that Smartans don't deal with?"

Imani blinks, then rests her head in her hands as she considers the options.

"That could fit in this." I take one of the cores out and slip the internals from the casing.

"You metabolise poisons." Imani stands and looks Raul up and down. "Anything corrosive would be an irritant more than a danger, and there's no virus you could carry without potentially infecting the whole ship."

"Nonlethals?" Rook muses.

"Exactly what they say on the tin." Raul shrugs. "We recover fast enough to mean that dunking our head in pepper spray has the same effect as mild hay fever for us."

"What about medicine?" Imani asks.

"Medicine?" Rook asks.

"Supposed to make us better, surely?" Raul raises his eyebrow, then looks down at the body on the floor. "Either way, I'd better get changed. Just hope I haven't got middle age spread after all these years."

"We also need to figure out what to do when we've got the distraction," Rook says. "We'll only get one shot at her before she goes turtle on us."

"I think I've got something." Imani nods, turning to face Raul and turning back instantly as she catches him halfway through getting changed. "How do you deal with indigestion, all that protein you have to eat to keep the muscles up?"

"You learn to deal with hard shit when you're a Smartan," Raul deadpans.

"But if there's too much hard shit?" Imani presses. "Regular constipation drugs wouldn't even touch your system."

"They wouldn't, no. You have to take something that would kill a normal person." Raul shrugs and checks the armour for tracking devices before clipping it on, tapping the pack on the leg of his other armour. "There's some in here, but you'd have to find a way to make it airborne."

"I can get around that." Imani grins. "Always wanted to make God shit herself."

"She'll still recover from it." Rook frowns. "What do we do while she's on the throne?"

"We reboot AL." I nod. "I'd rather be dealing with a truculent computer than a delusional psychotic looking to burn the universe down."

Rook pauses for a second. "How do we reboot AL? What if she's wiped out everything to do with his programming?"

"AL's hardwired." I tap the casing as I pull the core from it and hand the case to Imani to fill with Raul's drugs. "They had to find a way to ensure that a random EMP wouldn't wipe out the entire operating system; a lot of the programmers rebelled at the idea that we were using a switch decision machine as a reboot device, but it was the only method they could think of that would work in all cases."

"What are we doing while you're bringing AL back?" Imani takes the chemicals from Raul's pack and puts them into the case. "I need to build air pressure in this."

"*You're* bringing AL back." I pass her the pad from my arm and mark out the switches as I recall them. "And I'll need you to cover me while I bypass the bridge doors." I look at Raul as I take the camera from his old armour and fit it to the front of the core. "It'll only take me a few minutes, but if she's rigged the drones to protect her they'll keep acting as programmed till AL kicks back in." I pass the pad to Rook. "Memorise this; Imani keeps the hardcopy."

"How long should it take to reboot AL?" Imani asks.

"Minutes," I reply. "Unless she's rigged a bypass in the control room, which is why I need to be there. As long as we can put AL back in charge of the ship, everything will be fine."

"What about us?" Rook passes the pad to Imani. "What do we do when we've rebooted AL?"

"You make sure no one *unboots* it." I manage a half-smile, connecting the airline from the maintenance kit to the case and loading it with enough air to propel the chemicals within out when the case is detonated. "Raul, can you hold this closed while we get the seal on it?"

I hold my breath as Raul takes the case and holds the vent closed while I lock it down, only breathing when he nods and takes his fingers from the vent. Not a moment too soon; the ship lurches to port and we brace against the sides of the tubes.

"Someone put the brakes on hard," Rook muses. "Didn't think the ship could do that."

"It can't." I shake my head. "That sort of deceleration should tear us apart."

"It has before." Raul picks up his rifle. "It means we've arrived somewhere."

"Let's find out fast." Imani pockets my pad and taps her head. "Last three hundred times we arrived somewhere, they weren't happy to see us."

I trace the data cable on the side of the tube and run a feed to the viewer, making sure the cores are dismounted. The internal cameras would still need a programmer to break the encryption, but the external cameras don't have any security on them. I bring up the bow cameras, seeing the shining outline of the planet ahead, a single moon passing across its dark side. The ship slows and we hear the reconstitutors coming online, the power lines reconnecting throughout the ship as it goes to combat readiness.

Rook leans forwards, pointing at the base of the screen. "Can we move the cameras?"

"No." I tap the feed. "We can only look."

"Then wait…" Rook leans closer, unintentionally pushing us out of the way of the screen, his concentration absolute. "Something about this."

"Cloud cover, water covering more than half of the world, signs of vegetation, mountains… looks like it fits all the criteria," Imani muses.

"No." Rook taps the viewer again. "Look up, at the top of the world, coming into view now."

"They've got a station up there." I look at the construct

as it comes into range, massive, looking more like a launching platform than a monitoring station. "Big bugger. Could be this race has already managed to get into space, in which…"

I feel my throat constrict as the station comes into the light, the solar panels along the side cracked through long lack of maintenance, but sufficient power to keep the internal station lights on. The station revolves and the colours on the side become clear.

"Traveller." Rook jabs the screen with enough force to make it rock. "That's Traveller Station."

Imani goes pale. "Then that's…"

"Earth." It's a half-second before I realise the words were mine. "It's Earth."

Chapter Seventeen

"How…?" Imani watches as Traveller turns slowly in orbit. "The course we were on…"

"Was the first planet we came to." Rook shakes his head. "Who knows what course she plotted when she was done with the first planet."

"But if that's Earth…?" Imani looks close at the screen.

"We're about to destroy our Homeworld." I tap the screen. "We've got to stop her now. If we get AL back online, it'll stop all of this in an instant."

"Alright." Raul turns back towards us, rifle slung, the comm unit of his dead copy offered out to Rook. "We need to get moving. Stay on channel three; she only ever uses channel one."

The main deck is noisy; the constant clunking and whirring echoes through the halls, the combat drones not functioning as all efforts are diverted towards the coming drop to the planet below. We take longer than we should to get to the bridge, giving Rook and Imani time to get to the central core. Raul walks behind me, one step to the right, close enough to pull me out of the way, far enough away to make it look like

I'm his prisoner.

Not like I'd have a chance of escaping him anyway.

I keep my arms behind me as we walk to give the impression that I'm cuffed, the detonator for the core casing just up my sleeve. The bridge corridor is sealed; I hear Raul muttering something on his comms, then a muffled crunch as long disused gears mesh together, the light beyond shining through. A long shadow appears in the light, the misshapen head unmistakable. McClintock sashays forwards and raises her arms as if in benediction. The noises of the ship around us cease, replaced by the clicking of her boots against the deck and the quiet hum of the shield drone behind her.

"Do you see the futility of opposing me?" She looks me up and down, pointing to the floor in front of her as she looks at Raul. "You retrieved the cores?"

"I did." Raul steps forwards and puts the cores on the floor, stepping back to stand behind me again. "The other two are dead; this one chose not to resist the inevitable."

"A pity that they could not be here to see my final triumph." McClintock walks forwards, gathering up the cores, looking at me with a gleam in her eye. "At least they saw these. Tell me, did they understand the magnificence they sought to challenge?"

"Magnificence?" I stifle a smirk. "No, they didn't get that."

"How could they not?" McClintock steps forwards, a snarl building on her lips. "How could you look upon what I have achieved and not be awed?"

"Oh, they saw something." I signal to Raul behind my back. "But it wasn't magnificence."

"I suppose that such little creatures could not be expected to recognise greatness." The snarl turns pitying and McClintock sighs. "Tell me then, what did they see in me?"

I feel Raul's left hand brush against my thumb. *Good to go.*

"They saw you were full of shit." I smile and press the detonator.

The casing in her hand tears open and the inside of the shield is sprayed with the airborne mix of Raul's chemicals, momentarily obscuring McClintock from view.

"I hope you have something better than this," McClintock's voice echoes outwards. "You thought the supreme being to be defeated by mere…"

Her voice cuts off as there's a sound like a coffee machine with a burst feed pipe.

"Kill her." From the light behind her, I can see that McClintock is doubled over now, her voice strained. "Kill her and bring me my…"

Her voice cuts off again as she sees Raul slapping the EMP charge on the shield.

"Damn you." She turns and runs towards the light behind her; the field flickers long enough for her to go out of the back of it, the drone remaining in place as the bridge doors slam shut. The field shudders for a half second before the EMP detonates and Raul leaps forwards to hold the doors, bracing his back on one side while pushing with all four limbs against the other.

"Get through." His voice is as strained as his body as the door continues to close, the screeching of the machine shrill as mechanical muscles try to defeat their organic counterpart. I drop under him and scrabble through, coming up on the other side.

"Let it go." I tap him on the shoulder. "I'm through."

"Not so easy, Commander," he growls, shifting his left leg, then his right. "I didn't get far enough in, so if I…" His head goes down as he calls on several lifetimes of willpower. "If I jump your way, the door will certainly crush me. This is a journey you have to make yourself. Take my gun and my comms, and make sure we didn't get this far for nothing."

I take the massive automatic from his thigh holster and his headset. He nods, his arms starting to tremble as the machine starts to get the upper hand.

"Good hunting, Commander." He shifts both his legs and leaps away, the door closing in an instant.

Hope he made it.

I walk down towards the light; after more than a day in dark corridors, the flaring brightness of the bridge is almost painful to my eyes. The gun is at my side as I fit the comms on my head.

"Mara to Rook." I keep my voice down. "Are you there?"

"We're here, Commander." Rook mirrors my tone. "Did you get in?"

"I did." I pause as I clear the airlock to the top bridge, looking down on the triple command balconies, then over to the reconstitutor in the corner, long unused, the vat of powder above it the same one that we set out with all those years ago.

No better way of keeping a ship functioning than being able to rebuild injured personnel on the spot.

"Commander?" Rook, his voice deeper, an edge of concern there.

"I'm in," I say again. "Raul got me in, but couldn't follow. He's outside."

"We'll start the sequence now," Rook says. "Try and keep Captain Fruitcake away from the reboot controls. You'll know when we manage it; everything'll go dark."

"Are you both okay up there?" I go up to the second balcony, and everything is quiet up here.

Too quiet.

"We…" Rook pauses and I hear the unmistakable humming of drone rotors, looking around for a few seconds before realising that the sound is coming through the comms. "We have inbound, Commander. Look for the darkness; it's all on you."

"Be safe, both of you," I say.

"And you." Rook cuts the comms.

I hear the sound of the bridge toilet flushing.

Never heard it before because the bridge is always noisy.

I wait with the pistol out and draw a line of fire on the corridor leading to the toilets, waiting for McClintock to come out.

Headshot; bodyshots will only irritate her.

The sound of footsteps echoing down the corridor and I see the shadow shorten as she comes towards the exit. She comes around the corner, one hand over her stomach as her physiology continues to process the chemicals. My finger tightens on the trigger.

The lights go out and she gasps at the sudden darkness.

I pull the trigger.

Chapter Eighteen

The gun roars, the sound so much louder against the silence that came before. The flash illuminates the bridge, but no scream, no sound of a body hitting the floor.

Damn it.

The reserve lighting comes on and the centre console lights up on the third balcony. I don't look down to see what she's doing, but run for the stairs leading up. The sound of rapid footsteps below me tells me my shot didn't have the intended effect. I'm almost to the top of the flight of stairs when she catches me, her enhanced speed easily outmatching mine. We skid to a halt against the far wall and I kick out, catching her across the circuits in her head. She screams, not pain, rage, her eyes all but black in the low light.

"Weak creature." She rises up, her right arm hanging loose by her side, the shot having gone straight through her shoulder. The bleeding has stopped, but she's not focussing on it, so it's not healing like a Smartan. "Did you think to slay your god as you would a lesser being?"

"You're not my god." I stand up, trying to keep my distance, looking around for the gun.

"Oh, but I am." She moves to the side and I mirror her movements, both of us circling on the thick carpet of the command deck. "How many times do you think I have both given you life, then taken it back when you were no longer of use?"

"You?" I force a laugh. "You mean your drones."

"My servants." Her tone is sharp, a rebuke for questioning her. "A true god doesn't soil her hands in the mundane matters of her universe."

"A true god has the power to do things herself." I see the gun under the commander's chair and keep circling. "What have you done?"

"Did you not see the logs?" She pauses in disbelief at my question. "Have you not seen that I have brought order to the universe."

"You brought death to the universe." I keep circling. "What god only destroys?"

"Humanity now thrives on hundreds of worlds." She tries to spread her arms, looking down at the right as the left comes up by itself. "Hundreds of them. It was not man that took us to the stars, it was me."

"Riding on others' genius." I keep prodding at her ego. "Some God."

Her expression darkens at my disrespect and she draws a deep breath, closing her eyes for a second to compose her thoughts. I dive backwards towards the gun, sliding along the floor till I hit the commander's chair, picking the gun from the floor. I hear the running feet, far faster than mine, feel her hand close on my gun hand like a vice, her right still hanging useless at her side. She pulls my hand into the air with ease and looks down at me with contempt in her smile. I can feel the bones shifting in my wrist as she starts to turn the gun inwards.

Seconds before that's pointing at my head.

I grab at my toolbelt, pulling at the equipment there; she leans closer as the gun nears my head, close enough that I can see into her eyes.

"Do you see now that I am your god?" she asks. "Do you understand now?"

"No…" The word comes out almost whispered through the pain. "You're still… not doing it yourself…"

She looks down at me and I feel her hand moving along mine till her fingers are in the same place as mine, her index finger pressing against mine on the trigger.

"Will that convince you…?" She looks down at me. "Is that the proof you need?"

"Tell me something…" I grit my teeth against the pain. "My… god."

"A last request?" She seems genuinely amused by the notion, but her hand remains steady upon mine. "Never let it be said I am not a merciful god. Speak your request."

"Tell me…" She leans in close as my voice gets fainter. My right hand closes on the TacGel cannister in my belt and I bring it around slowly so as not to alert her, pulling the cap off so the needle is out. "Tell me why."

"Why?" She frowns. "Why what?"

"Why…" I slump back and she hauls me upwards, her arm pulling mine high. I stab upwards, the needle on the TacGel cannister penetrating her lower jaw as I force it upwards as hard as I can. The can gurgles and the chemicals spray out.

She staggers backwards, her hand releasing mine as her throat makes a bubbling sound, the air cut off in less than a second as the Gel expands. She reaches up to her throat with her one good hand, pulling at the Gel as it starts to harden, hunched over as she tries to draw air in. I switch the gun to my other hand and point it towards her.

"Why can't you shut up…?"

Even choking for air, she stares at me, her disbelief that anything would dare challenge her still defiant in her eyes. I keep the gun on her as she steadies herself against the balcony railing. Any normal human would have been dead by now, but her only thought is now the thing choking her. Raul's words come back to me.

The muscle follows the mind, what you visualise will happen.

Even as I watch, the Gel starts to dissolve in her mouth. She looks at me, air coming into her lungs slowly even as the Gel continues to expand. I shoot, not so accurate with my other hand, but she's distracted. The first shot misses, the second and third hit her in the torso and she goes to one knee. I keep my distance, firing again and again, each shot striking her in the chest. She stares up at me as, for the first time in hundreds of years, she fears her own ending. I bring the gun up to point at her head and her eyes widen. She struggles to stand and turns away, leaning on the railing. I hesitate, not willing to shoot her in the back.

Too late I realise her intent; she flips over the railings and falls two storeys to the deck below. I run over and look down, seeing her laid there, still moving. I reload the gun and start down the stairs.

"Mara, MARA." Imani's voice is full of fear over the

comms. "WE'RE OVERRUN, YOU NEED TO…"

I turn back as the comm cuts off, running back to the panel and flipping the override switches to bring AL back online. The reserve lights cut out, the main lights coming back up in an instant, the program loading as fast as it did when we first activated it.

"Betrayer protocol." I hear McClintock far below me, her voice rasping over the shredded vocal cords. "Captain Eve McClintock, all drones to my authority."

"Command override." I look down at her. "*Commander* Mara Loganova, Engineering Division. Stand down all drones and return ship to ready state."

A click as the program digests the two separate commands, extending for more than a second. I feel a nervous tinge in my stomach.

What if she wrote an override in…

"Command accepted," AL intones. "All drones stood down per your order, Commander."

I run down the stairs to where McClintock has managed to stand. Two of the bullets have been pushed out as her body heals, and her mouth looks burned, but there's no Gel in it. I raise my gun as she hobbles backwards, keeping it trained on her.

"You think this is the end of it?" She spits the words at me. "You think you are anything but a speck of dust to me?"

"No…" I fire again, the round knocking her backwards as I walk towards her.

"You only"—she stares at me, the hatred rolling off her in waves—"only have two bullets left."

"Only need one," I say, keeping the gun trained on her

head.

"You should save the last"—she groans as another bullet pushes out of the wound it made—"for yourself."

"And the other for you." I take another step and she stumbles back, her hand going to the wall to steady herself. Another shot and she bumps against the back wall, her eyes narrow as she realises I only have one round left.

All she has to do is survive the last bullet and I'm done for.

"Command override," I announce to the air. "Engage deconstruction protocol for injured crewmember McClintock."

"Understood," AL's voice sounds out across the bridge as a glass screen drops in front of McClintock, the reconstitutor cycling up, lights coming on all the way along the floor where she stands. "Deconstruction protocols engaging."

McClintock lunges forward to strike the glass, the impact leaving a bloody stain against it. She stares at me, then strikes again, her mouth opening to speak. A spark of raw power ripples over the chamber and her right arm dissolves into dust. The machine cycles up and the grid lights up on both sides.

"Don't do this." She presses up against the glass, her now eyes those of the terrified girl who started this so long ago. "Please, please, don't do this."

The energy wave starts to move in from all sides. McClintock presses harder against the glass, as if she could find a way to pass through it, banging relentlessly against it as the energy builds. She puts her hand out, spreading her fingers.

"You don't know what you're doing." All elements of her godhood have fled. "You don't have to do this. I'm saving the universe."

"So am I." I put my hand against the glass, mirroring her hand.

Her eyes roll up as the energy touches the back of her head and her body goes limp, collapsing backwards into the energy field. I bring my hand down as the wave finishes cycling and the door reopens. The only things remaining in the reconstitutor are the circuits boards that made up her head. I pick them up and put them in the recyclers.

Better that no one ever makes use of them ever again.

I thumb my comm. "Imani, Rook, where are you?"

No response.

"Imani, Rook, respond?"

No response.

"AL." I realise that for the first time since I woke up I can trust what I'm talking to. "Please locate Rook Layton and Imani Limbani."

"Both of them are located at the junction of vertical 25 and horizontal 17, near the master power relay," AL replies. "There are a significant number of drones in that area as well, all deactivated per your instruction."

"Life signs?" I ask.

"Inconclusive," AL replies. "Too much electrical interference to run an effective scan."

"Open all the doors between here and there," I say.

"I'm going up."

Chapter Nineteen

The bridge doors open and I look at the carnage outside. A field of broken drones is strewn before me, heavy explosives damage to the bulkheads and the scoring of lasers across all the walls.

"Commander." The voice is weak, but it carries in the silence.

I look to the far side of the room where Raul is sat against the wall, his armour covered in the oil of his enemies but mixed in with a deeper red liquid as well. He looks up as I get closer.

"AL," I speak down the comms, "medical drones to…"

Raul smiles and shakes his head. "Then we won." It's not a question.

"We did." I try to smile, looking over the holes in his armour, willing my eyes not to betray what I'm seeing. "We got her, but we can get help. We can keep you here."

"I do not belong here." Raul rests his head back against the bulkhead. "I have lived far longer than any man should, and I have done so for my duty, longing for a time when I would have to give no more to the future, and be only myself alone."

He coughs, a trickle of blood emerging at the corner of his mouth and I reach out, wiping the blood away.

"This has been a good life." His old eyes are fierce as he looks at me. "Here, and now, I can pass the future to one I know who will care for it as I have. It has been my honour to serve with you over these years, Commander Loganova."

"Mara." The words catch in my throat.

"Mara." He nods, lower and longer than he should, putting his hand on my shoulder. "You must go; the others need you more than I, and know that one day, we will see each other again."

I stand and bow at the waist to him. His smile gets broader for a second and he lays back, his eyes closing.

*

I run from the room, taking the elevator to vertical 25 and scrambling down the tube to horizontal 17. There are drone parts everywhere, the remains of the army that McClintock sent up here to stop them, and in the corner, two bodies, one atop the other, are laid against the switch array. I pick my way through the debris, hoping against hope for some sign of life. As I reach the bodies, I can see that the top one is Rook, his torso cored from front to back; he must have moved in the way to try and shield Imani from the onslaught, but nothing could have stopped that rain. I reach down, my hands trembling as I try to hold the tears in, moving to the side of them. Underneath, Imani lays silent, her arms around Rook's head. She must have been trying to shield him from the drones, both of them only thinking of the other.

I slump to the floor beside them, broken ragged howls tearing out of my lungs as I weep for my friends, the noise echoing through the tubes till the whole ship echoes with my sorrow.

I don't know how long I stay there, AL now cleaning the area around me, sweeping away all traces of what happened there. The drones, once so deadly, now repurposed back to what they always should have been. I see the medical drones hover close by, the stretcher suspended between the two parts of it.

"I detect no lifesigns, Commander," AL's voice echoes in the tubes. "I will return them to the vat for reconstitution; they will be as good as new soon."

As good as new. Yes, they will be, but they won't remember what happened here. They won't remember the wars we fought these hundreds of years, they won't remember us winning, they won't...

I nod in mute silence, waiting till I'm alone in the tube before getting up and heading back to the bridge. The main entranceway is cleared of everything.

Including Raul.

I pace slowly down to the bridge, looking up at the main screens. "Activate external cameras." I lean heavily on the console, waiting to see the world my friends gave their lives for.

It's beautiful.

Huge continents of green, vast oceans of blue, the wisps of high clouds and the towering peaks of the mountains emergent through them. I feel a tear of joy winding down my face.

Home again. It was worth it.

The nuclear detonation on the surface below breaks my reverie. I stare in mute shock as the expanding cloud erupts into the air.

We were too late; the ship is already attacking.

"AL," I shout. "Cease Protocol Four immediately."

"Protocol Four is not in effect," AL responds. "The munitions visible were fired by the inhabitants of the planet."

"What…?" There's a cold feeling in my gut as I stare at the screen. "How?"

"One moment." There's a whirring noise as AL's processor goes into overdrive. "Accessing Traveller archives; this war has been going on for more than three *hundred* years."

"Three hundred years." I stare open-mouthed at the screen. "But the people, the nations who fought those wars, they're long dead."

"Their descendants continued the war when they died. The planet has been at war since this ship left orbit; would you like to see the records of the conflict?"

"No…" I put my head in my hands. "No, I don't. Are there any nations where the war has not spread?"

"One moment." AL's cortex whirrs up again. "There are safe zones in each warzone designated as no combat zones; these are made safe so the generals of the armies can plan the war without concern for their own safety."

"And the other side honours this?" I look up in disbelief.

"It is an arrangement made between all participating parties in the Game," AL replies.

"Game…"

"The name given to the war," AL says. "Records show that the Colony Wars were renamed The Game more than a hundred years ago when the no combat zones were established."

"What of the general population?" I stand up and start to

pace back and forth.

"All life on the planet is purposed towards the Game," AL says. "Fertile humans are used to produce further units for the Game, then brought into the Game when they are no longer productive. It is uncommon for inhabitants to live beyond their twenty-seventh year, and the bodies of the fallen are recycled to provide sustenance for the Game."

I look up at the screens as another nuclear impact registers.

For nothing, all this for nothing.

I put my hands together in a prayer to a god I don't believe in, looking down through the external cameras, watching the destruction across the globe, the devastation, all so that people who thought themselves better than others could live easy lives while the world burned.

No change. This is why we ran.

I take a deep breath and my mind clears as I remember Raul's words.

There is no shame in regrouping.

"AL?" I look up at the screen.

"Yes, Commander."

I take a deep breath. "Engage Protocol Four."

I turn from the screen as I hear the machinery re-engaging, looking at the reconstitutor in the corner.

I don't have to remember any of this. I could just wake up like everyone else and see the new world.

I walk over to the reconstitutor and the door opens on automatic.

But then who would remember? Look at the world below; if we don't learn from the past, we're doomed to repeat it.

I pause at the door and make my decision.

Chapter Twenty

The deployment is half complete when I hear a throat being cleared behind me.

How he manages to make even a throat clearance sound proper is beyond me...

I turn to face him, dressed in two pieces of a dark three piece suit with the jacket slung on his arm, the tie done up in a perfect Windsor.

"Commander Loganova." He clicks his heels together and inclines his head enough to show the proper respect. "Deployment goes well, I presume?"

"Scarily so," I nod. "Initial scans show that the world's been through the wars a bit, but nothing we can't put back together again."

"Oh, there's a lot of things we can do down there." Imani leans in behind Rook and I see a blush spread across his face as she puts her hand somewhere it shouldn't be. "Right, Rookie Baby?"

"Plenty of animal life." I turn as one of the Smartans comes over, his rifle slung over his shoulder, the name tag reading 041 Abascal. "But nothing of those who made the world."

"Well, I'm sure we'll find the truth of it down there." I smile, stretching my arms back. "Look at it. If this isn't the promised land, I don't know what is."

"Always feels weird when you've just been reconstituted, doesn't it?" Imani rests her head on Rook's shoulders. "Like the mix is still settling."

"Yeah." I flex again. "Still, look on the bright side."

"At least we don't have to do that again…"

Discover Luna Novella in our store:

Lightning Source UK Ltd.
Milton Keynes UK
UKHW012135250422
402021UK00001B/84